Mrs Puchetti's Garde

J.F. Hoffman

This book is for my sisters

Table of Contents

Margarita stretches and rubs the sleep from her eyes. She spends her first waking moments making a mental list of things she needs to do before slipping out of bed, sliding her feet into her sandals and reaching for a shawl which she wraps around her shoulders against the cold dawn air. She takes great care to make as little noise as possible as she pads into the kitchen, leaving the sleeping forms of her family on the other side of the sheet that curtains the bedroom from the kitchen area. Margarita sets to her task preparing tortillas, some of which are for Alfredo to take with him for his morning snack on the building site. His new job is the first in months and would hopefully last as long as it took to erect the building ... perhaps five months? Margarita does a quick calculation. She has spent the money over and over again in her imagination. Alfredo is a good man. He does not fritter his wages on drink or gambling like some men. He brings the money dutifully to Margarita on a Friday evening and she gives him a few pesos back for a beer or a packet of cigarettes.

When Alfredo is not working, the family's sole income comes from Margarita who sells her tortillas in the local market. *Harina de Maiz* is plentiful and cheap and her tortillas are well known for their lightness and freshness. As the rest of the family sleep, you can hear the gentle slapping sound of the dough between her palms as she flattens and shapes the tortillas. Once they are cooked, wrapped up and placed her market baskets, she turns her attention to dinner. Assembling an array of ingredients, she spends the next hour making a big pot of chicken mole, thick and sweet, which, by adding beans here or a potato there, could last for three or four meals.

She will shortly wake Alfredo to oversee the children's breakfast and see them onto the school bus while she starts her walk into the town to take up her position, with dozens of others, on the pavement in front of the market. Here she will carefully set down her two baskets on a clean tablecloth, making sure the tortillas remain well wrapped in a damp kitchen towel to maintain their freshness.

The few pesos she earns will disappear quickly, spent on more maize flour and food for the family. A few pesos are put aside each week for buying fabric which Margarita will transform

4

into a pair of trousers for Jesús, a shirt for Miguel Ángel, and perhaps a skirt or blouse for Lupe. Margarita is determined that unlike herself and her husband who had never been educated beyond third grade, her children would get an education which would one day lift them from their humble beginnings. Any spare coins are put in a jar on the kitchen shelf for emergencies or necessities as and when they might arise.

Today Margarita sells all her tortillas and heads back home. As she negotiates the potholes, shards of glass and sharp stones on the dusty road leading back to the small compound, she occasionally gives her apron pocket a little shake to reassure herself that her day's takings are secure. Her home sits in a row of five dwellings, fenced off from each other by corrugated iron sheets which have rusted in the sudden showers of the last few rainy seasons. She eases open the makeshift door in the fence, a slab of metal advertising Goodyear Tyres. The squeaking of its hinges momentarily rouses a neighbour's dog from its slumber, and she makes gentle shushing sounds lest she should spark off a round of hysterical barking.

Margarita takes great pride in her home. Here, there is a place for everything. On the outside, hanging from a hook at the back, is a large, battered zinc tub. Pots and pails are ranged on the shelves made from planks of wood and old bricks which stretch from one end of the exterior of the shack to the other, interrupted only by the door-less frame. From this gaping hole hangs a piece of cloth, its gay stripes now faded by the sun, flapping languidly in the occasional puff of diesel breeze. Inside, you enter first the kitchen in which a large table takes up much of the space. It is covered with a plastic tablecloth, its sunflower pattern barely discernible in the faint light of a single 40-watt bulb. The table looks out of place here. It is solid and sturdy with a dignified air of permanence about it, in sharp contrast to the crumbling walls and tin roof which contain it. The table is big enough to accommodate six chairs, each different from the other, including a captain's chair which also has an authority and presence which is out of place here. A shelf above a butler sink holds crockery, cutlery and a small white radio, while saucepans are housed in the void behind a net curtain beneath the sink. All the cooking is performed on a two-ring gas burner. A bed sheet divides the room. Beyond it there is a larger space housing an old sofa, a fold-up bed and a large double bed. This is raised a couple of feet off the ground on a platform beneath which are several cardboard boxes crammed with clothing and a few possessions. The only natural light comes from a space in the breezeblock from which the hovel is constructed. This "window" is covered with a metal screen, almost blackened by dead mosquitoes and flies which had failed in their attempt to gain entry to the sleeping quarter, there to suck on the blood of the five bodies as they sleep.

As Margarita enters, her eyes need to adjust to the gloom of the interior. She sets the pan of chicken mole on the gas ring to gently heat up whilst she tackles her other chores. Before leaving for work, Alfredo will have filled the zinc tub with water from the outdoor pump and left it in the sun to warm so that Margarita might get a good lather up for her washing. She washes and rinses the clothes then hangs them on the washing line, checking it every so often to turn the sheets or re-position a shirt or pair of trousers to get the maximum benefit from the sun. During the rainy season she has to get the washing done and hung out as quickly as possible so that it dries by 3 pm when the rains would start and soak the lot. After all, life was hard enough without sleeping in damp sheets.

The laundry done, she turns to the preparation of the meal adding some beans and rice to the chicken mole and making some fresh tortillas. Margarita sings heartily, accompanying the ranchero songs which crackle tinnily from her precious radio. She loves to listen to the soap operas and the songs of love and loss. She carefully unwraps two large avocados and places them on a dish on the shelf. In fact, the avocados are over-ripe and bruised, but for Margarita, who has rescued them from the gutter behind a fruit stall, they are a prize which would be transformed into a creamy, cool guacamole to accompany their meal.

As Margarita busies herself thus in her kitchen, her husband, Alfredo, is in his death throes. Lying in the arms of Emilio Sánchez, his friend since school days, Alfredo's body shudders and twitches, his eyes rolling back in his head. His last sight is of the beseeching eyes of Emilio, the last sound he hears is the death knell of the scaffolding tubes which sway crazily three floors above him. Detached as they are from their moorings, the hollow clanging sound

6

they make can be heard as far away as the shack on the dusty road where Margarita smiles as she scoops the soft green meat of the avocado from its waxy skin.

Lupe, aged 15, sits on the school bus with her little brother. She wears her blue gingham school uniform, white socks and sturdy shoes, and her long black hair is worn in two thick braids wrapped around her head and secured with bobby pins. Miguel Ángel, four years younger, has the window seat and they play a game of "I Spy" as the bus trundles up the little side streets of the town dropping school children off on the way, before turning onto the mountain track leading to their home. It is stifling hot, but they have to keep the windows shut to prevent the dust from coming into the bus. Lupe's eyes widen as they pass the empty lot on which a new apartment block is being constructed. She sees in an instant the dangling, jangling scaffolding poles and the scene on the ground below. She lets out a cry as the bus speeds past. The men who are standing around the flailing body begin to drop their tools and run off, until only the body and the man crouching over it remain on what is now a ghost site.

"*Es mi papá! Es mi papi!*" she screams, pulling Miguel Ángel behind her as she lurches up the bus towards the driver who has reached their stop and already opened the door.

"Get Mamá! Tell her Papá is hurt. Run!"

Miguel Ángel, sensing the urgency in her voice, races up the dirt road towards the shack while Lupe flies down the road to the empty lot, scrabbling over rubble and broken glass. She reaches her father.

"Papá?"

She looks at Emilio who is crying and shaking his head. In an instant Margarita is beside her. Emilio runs for help, but Margarita can see straight away that it is too late. She touches her husband's broken body gently, a deep murmur starting up somewhere in her being. Then, as she holds him to her breast, a sound like no other erupts from her lips, a long wailing animal sound that comes from women during childbirth, or with the loss of a loved one.

The funeral is a simple affair, attended by Emilio, Alfredo's mother and his brother and Margarita's cousin Gustavo and his wife. The rest of the family live too far away and some can only be contacted by letter. With the exception of Gustavo most family members are as badly off as Margarita and would not be able to afford the fare to get to the funeral. Gustavo has paid for everything – the coffin, the flowers, the candles and a black car to take the family to the cemetery. Gustavo and Margarita had been raised together from infancy. Their mothers were very close, and even after they married they lived in the same lane where they shared chores and children. At 16 Gustavo went to Mexico City, like so many others, to seek his fortune. He started off selling *chicle* and candy on the streets, then, when he had enough money, he bought a second-hand Polaroid camera. He photographed tourists in Chapultepec park and the *Zócalo*. Within ten years he had acquired his own studio and did portraits of wedding couples, children in their Confirmation gowns, and school photographs. He had married a pleasant, bubbly woman, older than him, and unable to have children. Gustavo didn't mind. His business was his child and he poured all of his love and concern into it. Aurora, his wife, was good with the books and good with him, and that is all that mattered. He had always paid special attention to Margarita and her family. It was, after all, through his generosity that the children had their schoolbooks and stationery and the occasional treat and he had helped Alfredo and Margarita out with a few pesos to tide them over in difficult times.

A few interested villagers help to fill the small church. Aurora has taken charge of the children, holding Lupe and Miguel Ángel's hands throughout the service, while Gustavo supports Margarita. Jesús, the eldest at 16, his lips pale with unspoken rage, stands apart from everyone. If Margarita tries to go near him, he shrugs her off.

"Leave me in peace Mamá"

After the burial, the family return to the shack where they sit around the table, Gustavo positioning himself at the head of the table in the captain's chair. He is a dapper gentleman with a balding head and thick black eyebrows arching over kindly brown eyes. He wears a spotless white shirt and well-pressed black suit and tie. He removes his handkerchief from his breast pocket and wipes his brow. It is a stifling hot day, and the kitchen is airless. The sun is setting, casting a dusty pink glow on the breezeblock of the shack, but it cannot penetrate the gloom of

8

the interior, lit by the solitary bare bulb. Margarita looks at each of her children in turn. Jesús is tall, lanky, with his father's high cheekbones and strong jaw. The trace of a moustache is visible above thin lips which part to display two rows of white teeth in a smile which lights up his whole face. But not today. Lupe sits next to him with her wide eyes and neat, shell-like ears. Her bare neck and collar bone give her the appearance of a fragile bird. Men turn their heads when Lupe walks past. The hopping, skipping little girl of just a year or two ago now walks with a grace and charm which are all the more alluring because it is unconscious. The gentle sway of her hips and the outline of her breasts beneath her pinafore catches the eye of local lads and labourers and her steps are propelled forward in a rush by the shameful wolf whistles which rain down on her when she is in town. She sits now, eyes lowered, brow furrowed, as she breaks off small pieces of tortilla, rolling them into little balls and placing them on the plate in front of her. Next to her is Miguel Ángel, small and lithe, with a shock of black hair and beautiful dark eyes fringed with long lashes. He kicks the table leg and eats his tortilla in a desultory way, elbow on the table and chin cupped in his hand. Margarita spreads her fingers out over the sunflowers on the plastic tablecloth and, with her eyes fixed on her wedding ring, she talks in a soft, low voice to her offspring.

"I have spoken with Gustavo and our position is not a happy one. The architect, the contractor and the foreman of the project have, all of them, done a disappearing act. Obviously, they were building without planning permission or insurance for that *maldita construcción*," here Margarita stops to regain her composure. "So there will be no compensation, nothing. *Nada*". The word hangs in the still air over the table, as if in a bubble. "*Nada*".

"So, we must have a plan, because my tortillas won't be enough to keep us all for long. Jesús, you must finish the school year and have some technical training. Gustavo has kindly agreed to provide funds for your stationery and uniform and an allowance for you and your brother. And you, Miguel Ángel must also finish your schooling. I do not want my sons ending up labouring on a building site. You'll have proper jobs, in an office, proper jobs where you'll wear a suit and tie and carry important papers in a leather briefcase," she pauses, smiling through tears at her two sons.

Lupe looks up from her plate as Margarita turns to her. Her mother's face is ashen with grief. It is as if she has become an old woman in the space of a few hours. Her hair is even greyer, and her eyes are dulled by a film of hopelessness and despair.

"Guadalupe, I am sorry. You must leave school at the end of this term. Gustavo knows of a family in the city that need a *muchacha*. They're Americans, they'll pay you well. Gustavo thinks you'll do very well there, and you can come home whenever you have a weekend off."

"But Mamá," Lupe begins to sob, "I don't want to leave you. What will I do in that place? I won't have any friends, Mamá, please! Don't make me do this, don't make me go!"

Margarita takes a deep breath in an attempt to keep her voice steady.

"My child, if there was any other way, you know I would choose it. But short of leaving all of you to fend for yourselves while I try to find work in the city, I see no other way. Lupe, you're an intelligent girl. You have been a good student and a daughter your father and I are so proud of. Believe me when I tell you that for now this is the only solution to our misfortune. Gustavo assures me this family will take good care of you, and you must do all that they ask of you and listen carefully to the Señora's instructions."

Margarita stands up and goes around the table to where Lupe sits. She embraces her and holds her, looking down on the straight white parting on top of her small head. She rocks her in her arms murmuring endearments.

"My darling daughter, my life. You will be fine."

The next two months go by in a fog of despair. Lupe watches as her mother, bent by grief, toils to make ends meet. The dread she first felt at the thought of leaving behind all that is familiar to her has been replaced by a determination to do what she could, anything, to help her family. As the end of term approaches, she begins to detach herself from friends, from family, spending time alone as a rehearsal for the solitude she is about to endure in the big city.

The sun is just rising into a cloudless sky as Lupe and her family walk to the bus station in town. The bus belches out diesel fumes and the noise from the engine drowns out her mother's words of farewell as she embraces her daughter. They are early, so Lupe is able to secure a window seat and store her bags overhead. She watches as her family grow smaller and smaller until they are just waving specks in the distance and then disappear in the dust cloud thrown up by the tyres. The bus is laden with its human cargo and all the possessions that come with them. Inside, chickens, alive in baskets, gaily coloured serapes full of pots and pans, hessian bags overflowing with greenery and fresh produce. The roof of the bus is piled so high with bags and sacks, a cistern, an iron bedstead and a toilet bowl, that it is in danger of toppling over at every bend in the track leading down from the mountain. Those packed standing in the aisle hold on to the backs of seats or the dangling leather straps or each other for dear life. With knuckles white and feet planted as wide apart as possible, they sway to and fro as the bus continues its journey and finally judders to a halt at the end of a line of similar vehicles, their colours indistinguishable beneath a covering of red dust.

Lupe alights from the bus clutching her two bundles. She squints in the blazing sunlight which bounces up off the tarmac and the aluminium roof of the bus depot. There is a chorus of relatives greeting each other, crowing roosters, clucking chickens, barking dogs and children shouting as they chase each other between the bundles and paraphernalia now being unloaded by shouting men. A lottery ticket salesman sings out the prize to be won and newspaper boys call out the headlines. The shrill whistle of a chestnut seller pierces the stagnant air and the bells

11

of the ice cream vendor add a carnival feel to the cacophony of sound. Lupe, biting her lip, surveys the scene. She needs to take some deep breaths to still the rising panic within her. Then, towering over the crowd, a man in a cream suit and a panama hat calls out: "Guadalupe?". She raises her hand as if responding to a teacher at school. The man waves back, smiling, and snakes his way through the throng towards her.

"Hello Guadalupe. Sam Puchetti" he says, raising his hat, "I'm very pleased to meet you!"

"Mucho gusto Señor."

This is the first Americano she has ever spoken to and she wants to make a good impression.

He grabs her bags and guides her across the tarmac to where his car, a two-tone Chevrolet convertible, is parked. He installs her in the front passenger seat. He turns the key and the car purrs out of the depot and onto the main road into the city.

Sam removes a pack of cigarettes from his shirt pocket, pushes in a knob on the dashboard and, when it pops out, uses it to light a cigarette. Lupe watches, fascinated by this feat.

"Gustavo speaks very highly of you. I wish you could have come to us under happier circumstances."

He glances at her, hoping he isn't upsetting her.

"We were so sorry to hear about what happened to your father. It's a lot of change for you in a short space of time, but we hope you will soon feel at home with us?"

She nods, not daring to look at him lest she should burst into tears.

"Si señor."

He speaks good Spanish, which is a relief for Lupe. She shyly answers his questions about her journey, her village and her family and begins to relax a bit. They drive through the city sprawl, a patchwork quilt of barrios housing the very rich and the very poor, up wide avenues shaded by rows of palm and jacaranda trees. The radio on the chrome dashboard is tuned to a music station and they drive to the strains of "Volare". Lupe holds tight onto the strap by her window as if it could offer her an anchor in all this madness of smells and sights and sounds. The noise!

Presently they pull off the boulevard into a side road and then into a street lined with pretty white houses with red tiled roofs and more modern rectangular houses with large plate glass windows. Some of the dwellings on Avenida de los Picos are quite modest with small gardens and pretty balconies draped in bougainvillea, others are grander and stand in their gated grounds. The car pulls up in front of such a house. Lupe is taken aback by the sheer size of the place. Why there must be at least ten bedrooms in this house! Imagine having a bedroom all to yourself!

She doesn't have to imagine for long. Señor Puchetti takes her to the kitchen and out through a door leading to the garage. Here there are some stairs leading up to two rooms and an adjoining bathroom.

"Here you are Guadalupe."

Mr Puchetti ushers her into one of the rooms and puts her bundles on single bed.

"I hope you'll be comfortable. You must be hungry after your trip so please help yourself to a snack from the kitchen. I think my wife made some sandwiches for you and left them in the refrigerator. I'll leave you to unpack and settle in for the afternoon. The Señora will meet with you after her siesta and show you the ropes. I'll see you later on."

And he is gone.

Lupe busies herself unpacking her bundles. There is a small closet in the corner, a chest of drawers and a chair. There are some hooks on the wall by the chair and a gilded cross on the wall above the iron bed. The room even has a small balcony which overhangs the driveway leading to the front gates. Lupe hangs her few dresses and her coat in the closet and puts the rest of her clothes in the chest of drawers which have been lined with pretty paper with rosebuds on it. Two towels, a pillow, some sheets and pillowcases are folded at the bottom of the bed which she now makes carefully and tops with the embroidered bedspread her mother had made for her. The flowers and birds and butterflies so lovingly worked by Margarita bring sudden tears to Lupe's eyes. She quickly wipes them away, impatient with herself, and turns to exploring the bathroom with its own shower and a cabinet for her comb and toothbrush and soap. She has an hour or so before she needs to meet the Señora, so she has a shower, washing away the dust of her journey, and shampoos her hair. This she then towel dries and sculpts into two long braids each secured at the end with a small rubber band.

The closet contains four uniforms, three day-uniforms, two in pale blue and one in pink gingham with a starched white bib apron, and an evening uniform in black with a crisp, white, fluted apron. She would later learn that this one was for special occasions like bridge evenings or dinner parties. She puts on one of the blue uniforms and is surprised at how well it fits her. Her uncle Gustavo had written ahead to introduce her by letter and had included a photograph and details of her dress size for their information. She blushes at the thought of such personal information being relayed to total strangers. Lupe puts the finishing touches to her attire, giving her shoes a polish and tying her apron in a neat bow at the back. She surveys herself with some satisfaction in the full-length mirror on the closet door and then makes her way down the stairs and through the garage into the kitchen. Here Natasha Puchetti, Sam's wife, is at the sink rinsing out a glass. She is a striking figure, tall, slim. Her complexion is like porcelain and so pale in contrast to the gash of red lipstick on her delicate lips.

"Ah there you are Guadalupe! I am very pleased to meet you."

Natasha offers her hand and Lupe is a little taken aback by the firmness of her grip … almost like a man.

"Have you settled well into your room? Is there anything you need?"

Lupe nods and shakes her head in response, then follows the Señora on a tour of the house and gardens. Kitchen, utility room, breakfast room, dining room, living room, hall with a spiral staircase leading up to several bedrooms and two bathrooms. The house is bright and spacious, and the ceramic tiles and flagstones throughout keep it cool during the worst of the Mexican summers. Natasha points out the quirks of her home: a loose picture frame, the dodgy hinge on a bathroom cupboard, some wall hangings which will need to be vacuumed with an attachment. She also tells Lupe what her duties will be.

"You will prepare breakfast for the boys and el Señor for 7.30. My mother-in-law and I rise a bit later, so we only require a light breakfast … buttered toast with apricot jam and coffee, that sort of thing. I will leave it to you how you plan the housework and the laundry, but you will need to allow enough time to prepare the *almuerzo* in time for when el Señor returns at siesta time and the boys are back from school. You have one hour for siesta yourself and then prepare the supper. You will finish at 9 pm once the dishes are done and the table set for breakfast the next morning. You will have Sundays off so you can go to church, launder your uniforms and clean your quarters before having the afternoon free. You can have a weekend off to visit your family every six weeks."

Lupe tries to take all this information in whilst admiring each room and all the objects displayed therein. "This will take a lot of dusting!", she thinks as she takes in shelves laden with ornaments and statuettes and books … so many books!

The French doors in the living room lead onto a patio where a diminutive elderly lady sits. Lupe is introduced to Eva Puchetti who smiles kindly and welcomes her to the household before closing her eyes and resuming her nap. She is also introduced to the gardener, Pedro, who removes his hat as he is introduced to the new *muchacha*.

And so, Lupe starts her life in the Puchetti household. She works hard and feels tremendous pride when she receives her first pay envelope. She keeps a few pesos for herself and sends the rest of the money home, wrapped in a long newsy letter which her mother treasures even more than the money. Over the next few days Lupe gets to know all the members of the family and begins to feel more relaxed in her new role. She develops a routine of cleaning and cooking, with two afternoons also devoted to laundry duties. She especially looks forward to the days when Pedro is working in the gardens.

He is a bit older than her with a compact body and strong arms. He isn't what you would call handsome, like Arturo de Córdova or Errol Flynn, but he has a kind face and a beautiful deep voice. He works for the Puchettis on Tuesdays and Thursdays, having another job on the other side of the city in a similarly large residence. There he is gardener, handyman and occasionally chauffeur, in charge of valeting the family's two cars. On the days he works at the Puchettis he has a break at 11.30. He sits on a stool in the kitchen and has a sandwich or huevos rancheros or some soup with tortillas and cheese prepared for him by Lupe who has finished her cleaning duties and is making a start on the midday meal. The radio is on in the background as they chat about their work, their families, their lives. Every now and then a ranchero song comes on and Pedro sings along with his beautiful voice and Lupe blushes with pleasure as he sings the lyrics of love.

As they get to know each other she discovers his gentle sense of humour and admires his honesty and openness. One day, observing him from an upstairs balcony as he gently hummed a popular song whilst tending his vegetable patch, Lupe is suddenly suffused with an overwhelming feeling of love. Now, blushes come unbidden whenever they are together and her heart races in anticipation on the days he comes to work in the Puchetti household. Pedro meanwhile is taken aback by the feelings stirred when he observes Lupe from afar. Her shy smile, the way she tidies away a stray strand of hair, the nape of her neck, her sweet voice. They can't wait for the days to pass before they can see each other for their one half hour twice a week. But it is Sundays they most look forward to. They meet for a picnic in the park or go to the pictures or simply stroll hand in hand around the city centre admiring the shop windows dressed in luxury items they could never hope to buy. They embrace behind trees, in dark doorways, in the darkened cinema. Pedro always takes her back to Avenida de los Picos as the sun disappears behind the ring of mountains that surround the city. They linger at the gate and murmur their goodbyes.

"Until Tuesday, my darling."

"You will be in my dreams until then."

Lupe enjoys her daily routine looking after the family and household. On Pedro's days away she sets the sprinklers in the vast garden and hoses the flower beds and shrubbery. Pedro has instructed her to do this in the cool of the evening, and with her day's chores almost completed, she loves pottering around his domain, dead-heading flowers and clearing away fallen leaves and thinking about her love. She pays special attention to his vegetable patch which runs alongside the house. This is lovingly tended by him through the seasons to ensure the family has a plentiful supply of fresh fruit and vegetables. The neat rows of aubergine, lettuces, carrots, courgettes and tomatoes and the tubs of berries of all kinds flourish under his skilful hands. Herbs tumble out of pretty terracotta pots which adorn the whitewashed wall and release a heavenly perfume into the evening air. An avocado and a fig tree shelter the vegetable patch from the prying eyes of both Cha-cha, the family's Spaniel, and the Puchetti boys, Gregorio and Giovanni. This morning Lupe is gathering her dawn harvest. Armed with a pair of secateurs in one hand and a wicker basket over her arm, she picks the produce she requires for preparing the midday meal. Today the raspberries are plump and succulent, and Lupe intends to use them in a fruit compote. Pedro creeps up behind her as she bends to her task.

"Aha! Stealing my precious raspberries now, are you?

Startled, Lupe shrieks and jumps up.

"*Dios mio!*" she cries, holding her palm against her chest. "My heart!"

"Did I set your heart racing?" he teases. "Here, let me take your pulse."

He reaches for her arm and pretends to take her pulse with a comically grave expression.

"Hmm. This is very serious." He pulls her to him, and they kiss, sweetly, gently.

After a few weeks Pedro announces that for their Sunday outing the following weekend, he wants her to come to his residence in San Angel.

"The family are going away for the long weekend and the maid is going to visit her sister in Toluca, so we will have the place to ourselves!"

Lupe stays up late on Saturday to launder her uniforms and tidy her room. She springs out of bed early on Sunday morning and gets herself ready for her journey to San Ángel. She dresses in her favourite skirt and blouse and brushes her long hair, securing it at the back of her head with a tortoiseshell comb. She applies some pink lipstick and, putting her comb, a small mirror and her purse in her clutch bag, admires herself one last time in the mirror before setting off for the bus stop. She can barely breathe with the anticipation of being alone with her Pedro.

He is waiting for her as she alights from the bus and they walk to the house being careful not to be spotted by the neighbours as they enter through a side gate into the garden. They spend an hour having a meal at the table in the grand dining room. Pedro has prepared some cheese quesadillas, an avocado and tomato salad, and for dessert, a cream custard. He has put fresh flowers from the garden on the table and the radio is tuned to some music. Lupe can barely do justice to the meal. She knows that soon they will go up to Pedro's quarters and lie together on his bed. After weeks of secret embraces and caresses, of walking around the city locked together with arms around each other, Lupe feels as if every fibre of her body is straining for the touch of Pedro. She wants to feel the full weight of his body on top of hers and to engulf his manhood in her secret place. She knows from her own private explorations that this part of her can blossom and open, bringing forth a sea of warm liquor. She has heard the gossip of other maids relating their first experiences of love making … that it can hurt, that there can be blood, that they could be sore for days afterwards, that they could catch some nasty disease. She knows it won't be like this with her Pedro. The lovers gently touch as yet unexplored parts of each other. His fingers caress her as he kisses her lips, her neck, her nipples. She hardens under his touch and he knows when she is ready. Lupe opens to him and murmurs with pleasure

18

as he enters her, thrusting further and further inside of her. She holds on to him tightly and then as she wraps her legs around him, he reaches a place so deep inside her that she cries out with pleasure at the same time as he too reaches his climax. The rest of the afternoon is theirs and they spend it making love and whispering their dreams into each other's ears.

Lupe played every second of the afternoon back in her head as the bus home crossed the city to Lomas. When she got back to her room it seemed as if a lifetime had gone by since she had left it that morning, and she could not stop smiling as she remembered Pedro's body, his words, his kisses.

As their romance blossoms Lupe becomes aware of changes to her body. Her breasts become fuller and tender, a slight nausea and fatigue overcome her in the early evenings and finally, to confirm her worst fears, her monthly visitor has failed to appear ... twice. How to tell Pedro was enough of a dilemma, but how to tell her employers was a much more daunting prospect, and she didn't even want to think about how her mother would react. Would the Puchettis fire her on the spot? Would they put her on the first bus home to face the wrath and disappointment of Margarita and the pointing fingers of neighbours and friends?

Lupe knew she couldn't put this off forever. Her uniforms were becoming tighter by the day and yesterday Mrs Puchetti senior had asked her if she was feeling unwell.

"You are bit pale. Perhaps you are anaemic?"

She decided to tell Pedro the following Sunday. They would decide together what the next steps should be.

A Secret Shared

Chapultepec Park is bustling with activity. Families with picnic hampers occupy blankets spread beneath the trees and hopeful sparrows hop about waiting eagerly for a few crumbs that might come their way. Pedro and Lupe share the picnic she had carefully prepared that morning. The picnic basket is packed full with chicken and lettuce sandwiches wrapped in wax paper, cherries and grapes and tomatoes freshly picked from Pedro's vegetable patch, a nice ripe cheese and crackers and all of this is washed down with a bottle of Peñafiel lemonade which Pedro bought chilled from a nearby kiosk. Lupe couldn't put it off any longer.

"I have to tell you something ..." she started, and suddenly tears sprang unbidden from her eyes.

"No, you don't. I know. I know," he smiled his beautiful, generous smile and held her face in his hands, wiping her tears away and kissing her lips as they both cried and laughed and held on tightly to each other.

"Of course we must marry, and the sooner the better!"

Pedro went over to one of the balloon sellers and bought a balloon in the shape of a big heart. He knelt down on one knee before Lupe, and handing the balloon to her, took her other hand and said, "You already have my heart, my love, will you do me the honour of marrying me?"

Lupe blushed and smiled and nodded her head through tears of happiness. A small crowd had gathered around them and there were cheers and applause and much slapping of Pedro's back.

"Felicidades!!" they shouted.

They spent the rest of the afternoon planning how to proceed with this momentous, exciting and daunting situation. First of all they needed to inform her employers. Everything which would follow hung on their decision. Their lives and that of their unborn child were in the hands of the Puchettis. They decided that Eva Puchetti would be the most sympathetic to their plight.

She was always kind to Lupe. Perhaps because she came from an equally impoverished childhood, she had a certain empathy with this young girl from the country and took the time to chat to her as she tidied up or mopped the floor near to where she was sitting.

The following Tuesday Mrs Puchetti was sitting in her usual spot when Lupe and Pedro emerged from the house onto the patio. As soon as she saw them approach her, hand in hand, looking so serious, she guessed their news. She had been aware of the blossoming romance between the maid and the gardener. Whilst pretending to doze on the terrace during siesta, she had occasionally spied them exchanging smiles and once, kissing behind the large oak tree. She had lived too long a life to be cross or judgemental, and who was she not to wish them well?

"As for your employment, well I will need to speak to my son and the Señora. You do your jobs well and have become part of our family. Leave it with me and we'll see what can be done."

That evening after Lupe had cleared away the supper dishes, set the table for breakfast and retired to her room for the night, Mrs Puchetti talked to her son and daughter-in-law about Lupe's predicament. There was a lot to consider, primarily how Lupe would cope with her chores with a baby in tow. What about Pedro? Would he move in too? There was another room for servants next door to Lupe's room and actually Sam had been thinking of hiring a chauffeur. His mother was becoming less mobile with her bad hip and as the boys were getting older, they needed to be driven to extra-curricular basketball training, music lessons and over to friends' houses, tying him or Natasha to their routine when they had better things to do.

"That's all well and good," Natasha said, "but how does that help with all Lupe's work? There is still the cleaning and cooking to do, never mind all the laundry."

Mrs Puchetti considered her daughter in law's concerns.

"Pedro will help out until Lupe is back to her full capabilities. I have seen him helping her in the kitchen and he can be on hand to look after the baby so Lupe can get on with her work. I'm sure between the two of them this can work, and if for a couple of weeks the house isn't run like clockwork, so what? It wouldn't kill us to tidy up a bit and those boys have been thoroughly spoiled. It would do them good to clean up after themselves!"

Sam agreed: "The thought of finding someone to replace Lupe after all we went through to find someone so dedicated and trustworthy fills me with inertia! Having Gustavo's recommendation has really paid off, and hey! It might be fun to have a little one around the place again!"

Natasha weighed up the pros and cons. Certainly having a chauffeur was tempting and if the couple could cope with everything, it wouldn't impinge on her too much.

"So, we are agreed? She can stay, and with Pedro?"

Sam nodded his agreement.

"On a trial basis," interjected Natasha. "Okay then."

"They will be so happy to hear it! Natasha, perhaps you can discuss this with them? Lupe will appreciate it all the more coming from the Señora of the house."

Natasha waited until it was Pedro's day again so she could talk to both of them together. She came into the kitchen when Pedro stopped work for his lunch. Lupe rushed to turn off the radio, apologising to the Señora for the state of the kitchen with all the lunchtime preparations.

"Not at all Lupe. Please, sit down both of you," she said.

Natasha put her proposal to the couple. They agreed a plan and Natasha returned to the living room satisfied that, yes, this could possibly work well for her. Lupe and Pedro were ecstatic. They hugged and did a little celebratory dance after the Señora left the kitchen. To be together to raise their child and ensure the household ran on smooth rails was all they could want in life.

The next hurdle was how to tell Lupe's mother. They decided to consult with Gustavo and seek his advice. They met up with him by the kiosk near the balloon seller in Chapultepec Park the following Sunday. He was busy taking photos of couples on the boating lake or at the picnic tables. Pedro bought some cold drinks and chicken tacos and they found a quiet spot at a table in the shade of a plane tree.

"This is a bit of a pickle, isn't it?" Gustavo said, and looked down on the bent head of his niece. Her cheeks flushed with the shame of being such a disappointment to him. Pedro met his gaze. Gustavo immediately took to this young man. At least he was facing up to his responsibilities and he could see clearly how solicitous and affectionate he was towards Lupe.

"This is what we'll do. We need to put Margarita in the picture as soon as possible. Leave it to me to smooth the way. She may not be as angry as you think. After all she had Jesús when she was just sixteen!"

Gustavo was, as always, practical and non-judgemental. He suggested he write a letter to his cousin explaining the situation and then driving the couple up to the village the following weekend to face the music, with him as a buffer.

"But your work!" Lupe cried, fighting back tears, "Sunday is your busiest day!"

"One day won't break the bank! I can spare a day for my favourite family and, anyway, I haven't seen Margarita since Jesús' graduation. It would be nice to catch up."

A week later Gustavo picked the couple up in his car. It was such luxury not having to bounce around for hours on a bus! Margarita was outside pegging out some sheets when they arrived. She dropped the sheet she was holding into the basket and shedding clothes pegs from her apron pockets, she ran to greet them crying out and laughing at first and then burying her face in her apron to dry the tears that ran down her cheeks. She embraced her daughter, holding her tight. Then she held Lupe at arm's length to gaze at her child and lowering her eyes to the bulge that cocooned her future grandchild. She lay her hands gently on Lupe's belly and smiled through tears of joy. Then, looking serious she said: "You've chosen a tough road to follow, haven't you? You do realise this won't be easy. Gustavo filled me in on your predicament and your plans. You're a lucky girl to have such an understanding family. Most gringos would have cast you out straight away!"

"Yes, we know Mamá. God must be looking down on us to have such luck."

When Margarita heard her daughter say "we", she turned her attention to Pedro who was holding Lupe's hand and nervously biting his top lip. He smiled and introduced himself.

"*Soy Pedro, encantado de conocerle*–I'm pleased to meet you."

Margarita summed Pedro up in a glance. Kindly eyes, an open smile, courteous and respectful. Like Gustavo she warmed to him immediately, but put on a mock serious face and wagging her finger at him scolded: "Look what you've done! You should know that I'll be coming after you if you ever treat my daughter badly!"

She gave him an *abrazo*, planting a kiss on each cheek.

"*Bienvenido a la familia!* Come in, come in! You are welcome!"

Margarita proudly pointed out all the changes she had made to her home. The exterior was whitewashed with a new curtain hanging in the doorway and the kitchen now boasted a fluorescent strip light and a small chest refrigerator hummed gently in the corner. They all sat around the table covered with the sunflower tablecloth. They had freshly made lemonade and little cakes, candied almonds and beautiful ripe figs in syrup. Lupe and Pedro filled Margarita in on their plans and how they would manage her confinement and ensure the smooth running of the Puchetti household wasn't too disrupted. Margarita knew that dear Gustavo had a hand in negotiating the arrangements with his friend Sam and was relieved that he and his wife Aurora would be on hand, looking out for Lupe in the metropolis. She smiled her gratitude across the table and gave him a warm *abrazo* as they took their leave to return to the city.

The family were reunited a month later for the rather hastily arranged wedding in the village church. The gathering was small, just immediate family and a few close friends. They made their way down to the village in a procession waving to neighbours and passers-by, Pedro supported on each side by Miguel Ángel and Jesús whilst Gustavo linked arms with Margarita who clutched her daughter's hand.

The church had the heady smell of incense and a garland of bougainvillea mixed with sprigs of lavender adorned the front pews. The sermon was delivered by a new young priest who averted his eyes from the bulge of Lupe's belly. Anxious not to extend the time this couple lived in sin by a minute more than necessary, he made the sermon short and simple and before they knew it, they were out the door where their friends showered them with rice and a trio of Mariachis (paid for by Gustavo) led them back up the winding road to Margarita's house.

She and her friends Luz and Gloria had spent the previous few days preparing a banquet of chicken *mole*, *tamales* and *chiles rellenos*. A roasted pig or goat were out of the question, but the table was resplendent with different side servings of salads, frijoles and guacamole and other food brought by the guests. Bottles of beer and pitchers of hibiscus water were passed around and, once the mariachis had completed their hour's stint, ranchero music from the transistor radio made for a jolly backdrop to the feast. The newlyweds, still entwined by the garlands around their necks, sat at the head of the table whilst Margarita sat at the other end beaming and occasionally blowing kisses to them whilst also ensuring that her guests wanted for nothing and kept their glasses topped up and their plates filled. Following much singing and dancing and as the moon rose over the gathering, the guests began to make their way home. Gustavo and Aurora had booked a room for themselves and one for the happy couple in a small *pensión* in the village. Margarita ushered them into Gustavo's car despite their protestations to help clear up.

"No, no, no! Get out of here! I have a small army of helpers," she said, and sure enough both Luz and Gloria had already started on the washing up. The next morning, following a breakfast at the *pensión*, they made their way back to Margarita's house which showed no evidence of the banquet and festivities of the previous day. They chatted for a while recalling the highlights of the wedding day before packing the trunk of Gustavo's car with wedding presents and their garlands and setting off for the big city.

"*Adios! Hasta pronto!*" Margarita waved her apron and Lupe's brothers ran to the end of the dirt track waving them off. Lupe and Pedro waved out of the window until the car rounded the corner and headed for the highway.

Arturo was born the following October. A dream baby, he rarely cried, he slept well, and he ate well, and Lupe carried him on her back as she cleaned and cooked, humming lullabies and chatting to him the way mothers of infants do. Pedro worked out his notice with his job in San Ángel and moved in to the Puchetti household in time for the birth. Arturo would sleep in the hammock his father rigged up between two trees and Pedro too would sing to his son as he tended the flower beds and vegetable patch. On Sundays he and Lupe took their baby for walks in the park where they would have a picnic and go on the boating lake. They managed the childcare and their household duties between them. Mrs Puchetti enjoyed having a chauffeur to help her with her errands and visits to friends and even Natasha came round to seeing the benefits of having Pedro on site. It was a relief not to be constantly on call for the boys' social activities and it seemed that anything that was damaged or broken could be fixed by Pedro's capable hands.

Eva Puchetti sits in her living room. Her diminutive form is enveloped in a large, winged armchair, her head framed by a cushion and a lace antimacassar which hangs from the back of the chair. Her neat, booted feet are perched on a small footstool. Her thin hair, the colour of pewter, is swept up in a bun and secured in a black snood. Each lobe of her ears is tipped with a pearl to match the necklace wound three times around her neck. The room is dark, furnished in heavy, carved wooden furniture, the upholstery a deep maroon, the chandelier made from wrought iron and crowned with small maroon lampshades with gold tassels to match those of the cushion on which Eva now rests her head. The darkness of the room is not relieved by the large latticed French window through which she surveys her garden. She watches as Cha Cha her Spaniel, wakened by the clamour of the bell at the gate, leaps from the patio and runs across the garden to the gate where she makes menacing noises at the intruder on the other side.

The garden is like a small park. There are six trees, two palm, one jacaranda, two cypress and one old English oak, and there are flower beds colonised by exotic plants and colourful blooms. A high wall crowned with shards of glass from broken bottles – blue, green, amber and crystal – to deter intruders, contains the garden, interrupted only by the high gate with its spikes and a coat of arms. Above the patio in front of the French doors is a balcony. A luxurious shrub of bougainvillea covers the balcony and spills down the two columns on either side of the patio. Mrs Puchetti therefore surveys the scene like a play, the trailing bougainvillea on each side of the patio like the heavy purple drapes on each side of a stage.

Mrs Puchetti came originally from a village near Perugia in Italy. In Perugia you could walk down the cobbled road that goes from one end of the town to the other and looking up, see the beautiful frescoes on the ceilings of the rooms in the houses and offices that line the road. It is like walking through an art gallery, eyes raised, looking up at the windows of these buildings. Luckily the cobbles are so even and smooth for without looking where he was going, an enraptured pedestrian could have a nasty fall. Eva's little village seemed so quiet and boring compared to the bustle of the town and she looked forward to the occasional family outings into Perugia where she could purchase nice things and watch interesting people go about their business.

Eva and her husband, Rafael, had gone to the same school. They played in the village streets with the other children, and he would carry her schoolbooks for her, to and from school. He was like a devoted brother to her. If any of the boys teased her because of her skinny legs or fly-away hair, Rafael would leap to her defence and floor them with a punch, so they usually gave her a wide berth. Rafael's fighting prowess (and innate intelligence – he was always in the top three of his class) gained him the respect of the other children, and as an appendage to him, Eva too managed to avoid the worst of the playground jungle. Much as she loved Rafael, Eva was actually in love with Mario. He was the class clown, quick and cheeky, always with a clever retort to their teachers' remonstrations. One day a teacher launched a stick of chalk at him in frustration, and he caught it in his hand, bowing to the cheers of his classmates. He was sent to the principal where he received six burning whacks of a strap on his hand and was sent home for two days. Lessons were boring without him.

In the Autumn of 1911 with schooldays behind them and now helping to work the land and the olive groves with their fathers, both Mario and Rafael were recruited into the infantry and posted to fight in the war in Libya. Eva did not know who to shed tears for more, her best friend or her love. On October 23rd the young men were involved in fighting in Sciara Sciat on the outskirts of Tripoli. Even though the Italian troops had already surrendered, there was a massacre. Many of the men suffered the most brutal and inhumane torture by the enemy. Rafael escaped, but Mario didn't have such luck. Eva received the news when she overheard two women gossiping by the fruit stall in the market. She dropped the oranges she was carrying and as they rolled into the gutter the two women exclaimed in alarm as Eva crumpled and sank to her knees. Eva refused to believe that Mario's beautiful body which had enjoyed her caresses, his handsome face which hung over her even now, his soft lips, and kind, smiling eyes, lay crushed on some distant dusty battleground. She felt the walls of her village squeezing the life

28

out of her. Everyone and every place reminded her of Mario. S

war memorial with his name carved in the cold marble with the

fallen. She would walk out of the village into the orchard and s

and sob until there was no fluid left in her body and she felt

Puchetti, walking in the orchard, saw her thus, huddled agai

"I am going to America Eva, and you are coming with me, ...

and such conviction that she took the hand he offered her and smiling through her tears, said,

"Yes, I am. We are going to America ..."

They married the following year. Eva's parents wept throughout the church service and had little heart to enter into the festivities of the small reception in the village square afterwards. The wedding was just the first step to losing their daughter and perhaps never seeing her again. A few months later Rafael and his bride caught the train to the boat that, one month later, would take them past the Statue of Liberty to Ellis Island. Here they had their papers scrutinised and stamped, their baggage inspected and chalked, their bodies inspected and cleared of health issues, before being boarded onto a ferry to Manhattan Island and set free into the chaos of New York City.

They continued their journey to Boston where Rafael had some family. His Uncle Ernesto had a removals company whilst his cousin Elena offered them a room in the small boarding house she ran not far from the Charles River. Eva set about converting their room into a home for herself and her husband. The few sticks of furniture and a bed were all they needed at first, and Elena was happy for them to use her kitchen after the breakfast rush, once the lodgers had been dispatched to their various places of work in the city. With encouragement from his Uncle Ernesto and the remaining money he had received on discharge from the army, Rafael set to work. He hired a refrigerated cart and paid the proprietor of his local delicatessen to use a section of his large freezer. He and Eva spent the mornings making ice cream and he spent the rest of the day and evenings walking the streets of Boston pushing his cart, selling his home-made expanded to two, three, four carts, hiring friends and acquaintances as he

...s.

...t Rafael was out selling the ice cream, Eva busied herself with the day-to-day

...ry of keeping a home. Meals were basic, mostly pasta with a ragù and a tomato salad, or

...ick minestrone with crusty bread and butter. She was in the land of plenty compared to Italy. The shops here were an Aladdin's cave of goodies stacked high, but Eva and Rafael had their vision and saved every spare cent they earned to fulfil their dream of living in their own apartment. They had no intention of returning to Italy. Many of their compatriots who were working the mines or sweatshops would return to their villages once they had saved enough to rebuild their lives there. But Rafael and Eva kept their earnings to build their lives in this new world. The Puchettis embraced their host country, learning English, celebrating Thanksgiving and the fourth of July and displaying a small Stars and Stripes flag stuck in a plant pot on the fire escape. In the spring of 1915, with Europe at war, Italy joined the allies.

"You would have to be crazy to go back home now!" Rafael would exclaim to his fellow compatriots. "The war has taken its toll and there is nothing there for us, no jobs, no opportunities, nothing!"

Eva was in a constant state of anxiety, both dreading receiving news from home and dreading not receiving any news at all. Her cousins had been called up and were fighting in the mountains. If the enemy didn't get them, the harsh winter might.

The war seemed almost unreal, and their homeland was so very far away. The young couple pored over the evening papers and had heated discussions with Italian neighbours as they sat in their porches on balmy evenings. So and so's brother has been killed, and this one's father is missing in action, and that village has been devastated by bombs. Once peace came, Rafael and Eva sent food parcels, clothing, shoes and any money they could spare to help their families return to some kind of normality.

The war years were a struggle for the Puchettis' fledgling business. There was sugar rationing as the government encouraged its citizens to be more restrained in their food choices so more could be exported to the troops in Europe. However, when prohibition was introduced the ice cream market took off and sales soared. Drinks companies started to diversify into the ice cream business, but Puchetti's Ice Cream was a homegrown brand by now and Bostonians were loyal to it, especially as new flavours were regularly being introduced. Eva and Rafael moved into a one-bedroom apartment. Eva especially luxuriated in their own space, complete with a small kitchen and bathroom ... no sharing! And in 1921 she safely gave birth to their son, Samuel – "A good American name for my American son!" Rafael would exclaim proudly on their Sunday walks, lifting the little blanket in the perambulator to reveal his infant for all those he encountered to admire.

Rafael began to make plans to move his business on. Uncle Ernesto had been pivotal in sponsoring his nephew in his quest to come to America. He had helped Rafael and Eva both emotionally in their transition to American life, and financially in kick-starting the business. When he realised how well Rafael was doing, he used his connections in the business world to invest in his nephew, and with their backing and Rafael's innate business sense, the Puchettis were ready to take the next step. By now the young couple were fully immersed in family life with their precious son to look after, but they existed in a state of flux. People came into their lives and then one day they were gone, moving forward, moving up, moving back home, moving across the vast expanse of the USA to try their luck on the opportunities out West where the sun shone, and the fruit orchards flourished. Rafael and Eva became part of this flow of hope and aspiration. They loaded their furniture and chattels onto a cargo train and endured an endless train journey themselves across America to Mexico where land and labour were cheap.

Rafael and his backers had purchased a warehouse which, within a few months, was converted into a working concern and later a state-of-the-art factory. Refrigeration trucks carried Puchetti's Ice Cream to all parts of the country and across the border into California, Texas and New Mexico. Over the years the brand and its logo (a personified map of Italy with a smiley face eating an ice cream cone) were recognised throughout Central America and beyond. Rafael and Eva built their house in the Lomas area of Mexico City and sent Sam to the American School, taking huge pride in all his achievements, from playing in the basketball team to winning first prize in the "design a city" competition in his senior year. Sam was destined for a bright future, but sadly Rafael would not be around to delight in his success. Returning from a business meeting in Cuernavaca in 1945, he was involved in a collision with a bus on a treacherous curve in the narrow mountain road and was killed instantly. Sam was by now a qualified architect and just married to Natasha. His biggest regret would always be that his father never knew his two grandsons, Gregorio and Giovanni, and they never knew this extraordinary man who made something from nothing, including a family, which blossomed on the back of separation and grief.

Mrs Puchetti sits now surveying her garden. The bell at the gate rings again.

"Lupe!" Mrs Puchetti hammers her heavy walking cane on the flagstone floor.

"*Ya voy!*"

Lupe bustles out of the kitchen, wiping her hands on her white apron. She opens the small door inset within the gate and steps outside, out of Mrs Puchetti's view. A few minutes later she returns.

"Who was it? What did they want?" Mrs Puchetti asks, put out at having her siesta disturbed.

"Señora that was Teresa, the maid from the pink house up the road. She's heard that a new family is moving into the house next door. She says they are from New York and she thinks there are three daughters around the same age as Gregorio and Giovanni. They're moving in tomorrow."

Mrs Puchetti nods approval. She would look forward to welcoming this new family, especially the children. She smiles at the prospect of inviting them over to make friends with her grandsons and Arturo, and watching them play in her garden. How nice to have the chatter of three little girls in her ear rather than the boisterous shouts and barracking of those boys. Cha Cha pants into the living room and flops onto the cool flagstone next to Mrs Puchetti's footstool.

"Thank you Lupe. Would you tell Pedro to mow the grass tomorrow and perhaps you can polish the silver tea set, just in case our new neighbours can visit sometime this week?"

"We're moving to Mexico," Esther looked solemnly at Miss Brown, her fifth-grade teacher. Miss Brown looked down on the mass of black curls and the freckly furrowed brow of her pupil. Miss Brown had a kindly face, the sort of face you would expect of a Miss Brown. She reminded Esther a little of the Queen of England, but without the tiara. Miss Brown put a comforting hand on Esther's shoulder.

"That *will* be an adventure, won't it?" she beamed.

There was that word again. The night before, Esther's parents, Rose and Peter Jacob, had made the announcement at dinnertime when they were all sitting around the dining table enjoying Rose's macaroni and cheese, a firm family favourite. Peter cleared his throat, commanding everyone's attention.

"Something important and exciting is happening with my job!" he said, and they all turned to look at him., "I'm being re-located to Mexico City."

"What's re-located?" asked Dilly, carefully sliding a piece of macaroni onto each prong of her fork.

"It means going to a new place," Gail tutted impatiently.

"Is Daddy leaving us?" Dilly looked alarmed.

"Of course not!" soothed Rose. "We're all going together to live in Mexico. It won't be forever, just for a year or two, but it will be a great adventure and Daddy will enjoy his new job there."

The three girls took in this news. They sat in silence for a while, except for Dilly who pushed her plate away.

"I'm not hungry and I hate Mexico!"

Gail, Esther and Dilly are a popular trio amongst their village friends. Gail at 14 is slowly removing herself from the activities of her younger siblings. Her nose always in a book, she is top of her class in most subjects and a popular member of her cohort. Esther reckoned her sister's brilliance and glossy auburn *straight* hair was a real attraction for the *boys* in her class. Dilly , 5 years younger, is still a pipsqueak but a force of nature, winning the admiration of all the *boys* at school, and in the village, with her fighting spirit and sporting prowess … she could beat any of them in a race and was always picked for team sports. She has beautiful silky long *straight* hair which Esther loves to brush when her sister allows it, which isn't very often. Esther, now 11, lives in a bit of a dream world. She struggles at school, bringing home report cards which place her in the lower half of her class whilst her sisters bring home certificates and glowing reports. She is self-conscious about her looks ... especially her curly hair and freckles. So, although she thinks a lot about *boys* she is painfully shy around them and always feels a bit on the outside of things. Each of the sisters reacts differently to the news of their momentous move. Gail worries about the change of schools and whether they would sell books in English in Mexico. Rose reassures her on that matter but also makes a mental note to purchase full sets of the classics to ship to their new home, just in case. Dilly wonders whether she would still be able to watch baseball matches on the TV with her Dad. When she looked up "sports in Mexico" in her World Book Encyclopedia, it mentioned baseball, and something called *jai alai* and even bullfighting! As an animal lover she doesn't like the idea of that at all, but her Dad told her they do a lot of horse-riding in Mexico and she really likes the idea of being around horses.

Now as Esther sat in Miss Brown's classroom, she decided she didn't particularly want an adventure. She wanted everything and everybody to stay exactly the same. She loved the village she lived in with her family. It had been purpose built to house the hundreds of families who were from all corners of the globe , having left their homes to join the fledgling United Nations. The estate was made up of a series of grass covered "courts" around which the low-rise apartment blocks were ranged. At the back, most of the apartments had a small porch area and looked out over either a large grassy communal area or a playground. The children played outside in all seasons. Esther and her sisters would play hide-and-seek or Red Rover in the summer or build snow forts in the huge drifts of the January blizzards and wage war with the gang in their "court" against the gang in the next "court", snowballs flying in every direction. As Miss Brown droned on with the geography lesson, Esther day-dreamed about returning to her house after such a snow fight, numb with cold, and soaking clothes, she would sit with her sisters at the dining table, sipping a mug of hot chocolate, whilst scarves and hats and mittens dried out on the radiator in the hallway filling the house with the heady smell of mothballs. Esther's mother would float a marshmallow on top of their cocoa. The girls would laugh at each other as they lifted their faces from the steaming mugs, displaying a white moustache of melted marshmallow.

Miss Brown drew a mountain on the blackboard using white chalk. Then she used coloured chalk to fill in the peak of the mountain in red, and she made yellow sparks come out of the hole in the top of the mountain.

"Today we are going to learn about VOLCANOES," she said, and spelt the word in big red capitals on the board and the class copied it into their exercise books. Miss Brown then opened a big book called *Our Friendly Earth* and showed the class glossy, coloured pictures of volcanoes, some dormant, some semi-active, and some alarmingly active.

"And this one," she said, pointing to a snow-capped mountain, "this is Popocatepetl and does anyone know where that is?"

Miss Brown paused for dramatic effect whilst thirty pairs of eyes looked to her for the answer. "It's in Mexico, the country that Esther is going to live in!"

Esther sat stunned, her eyes wide with panic. A vision of herself and her family running away from flaming, sparking, boiling, oozing lava flashed before her. Did her parents realise the danger they were facing? The wrath of Popocatepetl would envelope them as soon as they stepped off of the plane!

Miss Brown had not meant to alarm her. She smiled kindly at Esther. She thought she had made her feel important in the eyes of her classmates who now gazed at her with renewed respect.

The months went by and Esther put all thoughts of Mexico out of her mind. Like most 11-year-olds she lived in the moment and she was far too busy with the Summer of 1961 to concern herself with worries about a major life change.

"Today I have decided that we are going to put on a play," said Amy, who was issuing instructions for the afternoon's activity.

The children were gathered in the shade of a huge oak tree. They sat or lolled about on each other in the long grass. It was very hot and humid, and they had been roller-skating all morning. They had gone home to make peanut butter and jelly sandwiches and a pitcher of grape flavoured Kool Aid before reuniting for a picnic lunch under the tree.

"Esther will be Princess Leonarda, Kim will be the prince, Katie, you'll be the dragon witch and Sophie is your husband. Gail will be the Queen and Dilly will be the drunk duke."

"What about us?" Jason and Douglas asked, one blond, the other dark, waiting for their instructions.

"You two," ordered Amy, "are in charge of props and sound effects."

The afternoon passed. The village was filled with the sound of cicadas, buzzing insects, slamming screen doors and the chatter and laughter of children immersed in play. At four o'clock the sultry stillness of the air was punctured with the sound of bells.

"The ice cream man!" they shouted.

The group of children beneath the oak, some by now festooned in costumes made from remnants of old curtains, sheets, scarves, anything floaty in fact, all scattered as if a firecracker had been launched into their midst. They ran off in all directions to their houses to collect nickels, dimes and quarters for the ice cream man. Then they ran down the grassy hill to the road below where the gleaming white truck stood, the sun glancing off the polished chrome of the fenders and the jingling bells. The "Good Humour Man" had a money dispenser around his waist. He would take their coins, inserting them in the nickel, dime or quarter section and dispense the change.

"I'll have a double whammy."

"Give me a baked Alaska."

"I'll have a fudge bar."

The door in the side of the truck would open letting out a cloud of frozen air as the "Good Humour Man" dispensed the ice cream into the eager hands of his customers. Then he would ring the bells, like Christmas bells in the middle of July, and call out "Next!".

Esther loved the "Good Humour Man", dressed as he was in his immaculate white suit and his white hat with his dazzling silver money holster. She vowed that one day she would marry a "Good Humour Man", that was if she wasn't married to Douglas already.

Then it was back under the tree to eat their ice cream and put on their production which would go on until suppertime. After supper, with the daylight stretching till nine or ten o'clock, the gang would re-group for a game of tag or Red Rover before being called in to bed.

Esther and her sisters were having supper one evening at the end of July. They were sitting on the little terrace outside their back door. At that time of year everybody ate out. It was too hot to cook indoors. Barbecues and salads were the order of the day.

"Girls, the moving men are delivering boxes tomorrow and you will need to sort out what you want to take with you," their mother said, speaking in a calm, gentle voice.

Esther and her sisters looked at each other. So, it was really happening, they were really going. The neighbourhood gang did not play Red Rover or tag that evening. They congregated under the oak tree and talked about the Jacobs leaving New York, leaving the village. They talked about the nature of change, transitions, and being left behind. The three sisters sat down with their parents to make lists of what they could take and what they would need to leave behind in storage.

"At least if it's in storage we have to come back for it," reasoned Gail.

"But that could be in years," wailed Esther, "and by then Douglas will have married someone else!

Rose had been obsessed for months with the family's big move. She had filled two office notepads with lists and notes with page headings in capitals: HEALTH, INSURANCE, STORAGE, REMOVAL, SCHOOL, TRAVEL and a page for each member of the family. The HEALTH page actually ran into pages with subheadings for "Immunisation" and "Addresses for Medical Practices and Dentists", and cuttings from newspapers about water purifying and how to avoid typhoid and cholera. The lists danced in her head as she fell into a fitful sleep each night and she could often be found at dawn at the kitchen table, poring over them with a mug of tea in one hand and a pen, poised in the other. She fretted over how she would manage to pack up the whole family and the contents of the apartment *and* make arrangements for at least temporary accommodation and schooling once they arrived in Mexico. She and Peter spent hours after the girls were in bed, planning this upheaval in their lives.

Rose and Peter were not unfamiliar with disruption in their lives. They had come to New York from a war-weary London. They had endured years of separation, each travelling the length and breadth of Britain to join their respective units in the RAF and WAAF. They wrote to each other sometimes twice a day and managed to wangle weekend passes every few weeks so they could meet up somewhere between their two stations. Travelling back to base after such a tryst was sheer torture, not least because the trains took hours and the weather was to say the least, typically British, freezing cold, foggy or pissing down with rain. Their letters to each other are full of yearning and love. They married as soon as the war was over and following a year or so training to be a surveyor, Peter had secured a job with the infant United Nations and he and his new bride were full of hope at the possibilities the New World had to offer.

"We're going to Yankeeland!" was one of the entries in Rose's diary for that year. One fogbound November day they boarded the boat train at Waterloo Station waved off by their entire family all calling out last minute instructions from the platform.

"Write as soon as you land!"

"Don't come back with a Yankee accent!"

"Send nylons and lipstick!"

"God bless! Take care! Safe journey!"

The air was full of soot and smelled of creosote. The train wheezed and whistled as it left the station sending a plume of steam and smoke from its stack. Rose focussed on her mother's face. Waving one of the lace hankies her sisters had given her as a farewell gift, she was suddenly overcome with a wave of homesickness and dread. What was she doing leaving everyone she loved and going into the unknown? She cried all the way to Southampton and went up the gangplank of the *Isle de France* with puffy eyes and a soaking handkerchief clutched in her hand.

As it was still kitted out as a troop ship, the sexes were segregated, and Rose shared a berth with three other "Yankee brides" whilst Peter shared his cabin with just one other gentleman. Nonetheless the liner aspired to the elegance and luxury of its former days, and they dressed formally for dinner and were entertained in the lounge afterwards with dancing to a big band or playing bingo or bridge or watching vaudeville acts from the time. A week later, on a sparkling New York morning, they stood on deck as the *Isle de France* slipped past the Statue of Liberty and watched lower Manhattan rise up before them. The liner was flanked by small pleasure boats and fire boats sounding their sirens and playing the fountain of water from their hoses into the sky by way of a greeting. They berthed at a pier and when the engine stopped the sounds from the city began to assail their ears. Honking cars and sirens and shouting longshoremen and the trundle of distant trains and buses.

Suddenly they were thrust into an alien world of plenty. After the privations of years of rationing, Rose watched as a sailor threw a half-eaten piece of pizza into the gutter from a bus window and the women on the pavements wore silk scarves and fur coats. Peter and Rose were one of several couples who had sailed over to join the United Nations. They boarded a bus with the UN flag displayed on its windscreen and made their way through Manhattan and onto Long Island to Lake Success where the UN was being housed temporarily whilst its permanent site was being prepared for what would become the iconic Secretariat Building in Manhattan. A village was also being purpose built for UN families and returning veterans in the heart of Queens. Racial discrimination at the time prevented these foreign newcomers from finding a home in Manhattan, so the village solved the problem of where to house all these people from all corners of the world. Peter and Rose soon settled into their new home and, with sparse funds, furnished their apartment and started their family. They formed strong friendships with neighbours and work colleagues who, like them, were young, idealistic, and starting family life in the village far away from their homelands.

So having survived the wrench from family and friends back home, the move to Mexico offered them and their family an opportunity to see a bit more of the world, daunting though the prospect was, especially for Rose.

Calery, Apartment 4, was near the busy intersection of two main roads: Ejército Nacional and Guttenberg. The apartment block, with its dark corridors and marble floors and walls, had a funereal air about it, not lightened by the depression that descended on the Jacob family as they attempted to assimilate themselves into this foreign place.

They always knew when they were approaching Calery because on the corner of this intersection there was a food outlet selling take-away chickens cooked whole on spits. The shop boasted a huge luminous sign "*Pollos*" above its entrance. It was made up of a series of twinkling gold lightbulbs like those you saw in Hollywood outside the movie houses. "*Pollos*" – chickens. The sisters mispronounced it "Polos" not yet realising the nuances of the Spanish pronunciation of the double "L" – "Poyos". The sign was like a beacon, a fudge of gold light from a distance, the lettering becoming clearer and brighter as one approached the intersection. "*Pollos*" and they were home.

Esther felt as if she was living in a dream world, that she would wake up and find herself back where everything was familiar and safe. The apartment was full of heavy old furniture and pastoral scenes hung on all of the walls in elaborately carved wooden frames. It had a distinctive musty smell which years later would evoke a great nostalgia in Esther, the smell of foreignness, of change. It was in fact the smell of the gas from the gas cylinders (which were delivered every couple of weeks) intermingled with the smell of boiling milk. Rose was frantically boiling and purifying everything her family consumed to protect them from the dreaded diseases she had read about. Even though they had all bared their arms and buttocks over a period of six weeks to Dr Geller's typhoid and cholera injections, Rose was leaving nothing to chance. Hence the milk was boiled and tasted and smelled so disgusting that no-one would drink it. The fruit and vegetables were soaked in purified water, giving them a faintly bleached aftertaste, and enormous bottles of purified water were delivered to the apartment and installed upside down in a water cooler, gurgling and bubbling up every time someone helped themselves to a drink.

Esther, Gail and Dilly huddled together, penned in by the sheer strangeness of their new world. There were no friends to play with, no one spoke their language and the streets were a cacophony of sounds and smells which were so alien to them. By day the cries of the street vendors wafted up through the windows of their apartment whilst late at night the lone eerie whistle of the "*serrano*", the night-watchman on his rounds pierced the silence letting the local population know that all was well.

For the first time in her life Esther had a room of her own. She at once luxuriated in it and feared it, so accustomed was she to her sisters breathing with her through the night. More often than not she would pad down the hallway into the room her sisters shared to be found by her mother in one of their beds in the morning.

The weeks sped by and in September the sisters started school. They stood in the playground like three statues whilst the other children surrounded them pointing and laughing and asking questions which the girls could not understand and did not have the language with which to respond. *El Director* stood on a small stage and silence fell as the pupils faced him to sing the Mexican national anthem. Over the weeks that followed Esther and her sisters would be able to join in a little bit more each day as they strung the series of sounds together until they reached an approximation of the real thing.

Esther was put into class 6B. The classroom was a vault of a space with a high ceiling and windows high up the walls, affording no view whatsoever other than that of the blue sky and the occasional puff of cloud. The desks were ranged in eight rows of five with Esther sitting at the front under the watchful eye of her teacher. She sat through days and weeks of total incomprehension. The teacher was able to relay only her frustration and anger to Esther who could not make out what was expected of her. Given a page of sums, she knew she had to add or subtract, and given some paper and colours she knew she had to draw, but history, language, geography and science were a total mystery, and she withdrew into her imagination and waited until recess when she could re-join her sisters in the playground.

The school was a fair distance from their apartment, so Peter drove them to school on his way to work. Esther sat in the back of the car between Gail and Dilly. Their father would drive them past beautiful houses, through parks with their statues and fountains and then, as they neared the school their father would shout out

"Here it comes. Ready, steady, now!"

And the three girls would chant: "Calle de los Amore! Calle de los Amores!" as they swung into the Street of the Lovers.

By Christmas it was as if a veil had been lifted from the Jacob family. They had moved into a house in Lomas and the headmaster of the British School had managed to accommodate the girls into three classes. The move to an unfurnished house meant that their furniture and belongings could be shipped and installed. Esther rejoiced in this reunion with all their bits and pieces – the sheets and towels, her own bed, her books and toys. Her bedroom smelled of fresh paint and floor polish, and from her window she could watch the sun set over the beautiful ring of mountains which encircled Mexico City. Elena was engaged as the live-in maid upon the recommendation of one of Peter's work colleagues. Like Lupe, Elena loved listening to music and soap operas on a transistor radio which she kept out of harm's way high on the kitchen shelf above the counter. Over the weeks and months ahead, Esther would spend some time each evening with Elena as she went about her kitchen duties washing up supper dishes and cleaning the kitchen surfaces and floor. Esther would sit at the big kitchen table doing her homework. She tried to learn the ranchero songs and they would sing along together. Sometimes Esther tried to teach Elena how to say things in English and of course her own Spanish improved greatly. Although Esther is much younger, she reminds Elena of her little sister and loves listening to her stories about school and all her friends. She giggles into her apron whenever Esther teases her about her boyfriend, Mario, feigning passionate embraces and making kissing noises. Sometimes Rose intervenes, coming into the kitchen to see what all the noise is about and sending Esther up to her own room where she will concentrate better on her homework.

"*Hasta mañana*!" Esther calls as she pushes the swing door open.

"Goo nigh!" giggles Elena, delighted with her proficiency in speaking English.

"*Arturo, cariño! Ven acá! Rápido, ánde, ánde!*" Lupe claps her hands and opens her arms as her son runs off laughing in the opposite direction with Cha Cha in hot pursuit.

"Arturo. Enough! Papá needs some help with the shopping, he's at the gate, hurry."

Arturo, almost 5 now and all arms and legs, races for the gate and opens both doors to allow the black saloon car to glide down to the garage at the end of the drive. Two youths tumble out of the back seat, hitting each other and laughing. Pedro goes around to the passenger seat and holds Mrs Puchetti's walking stick as he helps her out of the car.

"*Ya basta!*" Mrs Puchetti remonstrates with her grandsons as she slams the car door.

"I am fed up with all of this horseplay. Now help Arturo take the shopping into the kitchen. Gregorio, Giovanni!" she pounds the driveway with her walking stick as they ignore her, running into the garden and passing an American football over the flower beds at each other, their whoops and laughter bouncing off the trunks of the trees.

"Those boys," she mutters, shaking her head at Arturo. "So spoiled!"

Arturo is now diving into the trunk of the car, retrieving parcels. For such a slight frame he is able to carry almost as much as a grown man. He and Pedro take the shopping through the garage into the kitchen. Lupe is at the stove. She is nursing slight cold and is brewing up some mixture of herbs and grasses and twigs.

"What do these modern doctors know?" she shrugs. "This is good enough for my mamá, it's good enough for me."

Father and son put the parcels down on the kitchen table. On a sideboard a small white radio with an illuminated dial spouts forth the sound of a woman crying and a man shouting. Lupe's radio is her constant companion in the kitchen. She would peel the potatoes and make the tortillas to "*El Mundo Como Es*" or "*Tiri, Hija Del Amor*", and she would beat the eggs for *huevos rancheros* or dice an onion for the *frijoles refritos* whilst belting out a heartfelt love song with all the catches in her voice that she could muster. Today, with her dry, tickly throat, she does not sing.

"*Pobrecita*," soothes Pedro, putting his arm around her. "What can I do to help?"

Lupe sighs and tucks a stray lock of hair behind her ear.

"Señora Puchetti has invited over that new family from next door this afternoon. I want you to set up the garden furniture on the patio and help me to carry out the food. Arturo you can help your Papi. After that you can play with the others, okay?"

At this Arturo's face brightens. He loves playing with Giovanni and Gregorio. They are so big and strong, and they play all their games with such passion and dedication. He is their mascot. They don't mind him joining in and he is useful when it comes to retrieving tennis balls or shuttlecocks.

At three o'clock Rose Jacob arrives with her three daughters and Mrs Puchetti greets them from her chair on the terrace. The girls are delighted that Mrs Puchetti has a dog who helps break the ice with Gregorio and Giovanni. They pet Cha Cha and throw a ball for her to chase. Soon the children are all joining in in a game of hide and seek, leaving the adults in peace. At first the two women are rather formal but cordial. Mrs Puchetti serves the tea with her best silver tea service. It is not very often that she entertains, but when she does, it has to be done properly.

"Señora Jacob, you will have some biscuits? They are delicious."

Rose helps herself to an almond biscuit.

"These are beautiful! Where do you buy them?"

"From a little bakery in Polanco, not far from here. You must come with me next time I go. It is such a lovely bakery with a tearoom."

"Thank you. I would like that," smiles Rose, warming to her host.

Even after six months living in Mexico, Rose is still finding her feet. The children are, at last, happily settled in school with new friends and Peter is at work all day with his colleagues. She is at home learning how to be a "Señora" with a maid she does not want and very little other company. Life here compared to New York is so formal. No one just dropped in. You had to issue

47

or wait for an invitation , and even then you had to be fashionably late ... at least one hour after the appointed time! Rose is getting to know the customs and getting used to her daily routine, but she knows that she would never, never get used to the poverty she witnesses all around her. The area they live in is affluent enough, with large houses surrounded by high walls. But even here there are vacant lots where large families house themselves in shacks made from plasterboard and corrugated metal. There is no electricity, no running water and little furniture. Families all sleep, eat, argue and couple in one room. They bathe in a tin bath with just a bit of tarpaulin protecting them from the prying eyes of passers-by who peer over the breezeblock walls, their curiosity roused by the sound of children giggling, crying, whining, dogs barking and above all this, a mother shrieking at one or other of her offspring.

Rose watches as Mrs Puchetti pours the tea from the silver teapot which no doubt had attained its high polished lustre at the hands of the maid Lupe, or worse, her little boy. The women watch the children play and Mrs Puchetti is able to tell Rose about the best butcher, the finest wine merchant and the most convenient grocery store in the area. As the sun sets, Rose and her daughters take their leave. The girls are reluctant to give up their game with Gregorio and Giovanni. Mrs Puchetti walks them to the gate.

"You come over, any time you like. Do not wait for an invitation. Treat this as your home ... *es su casa!*"

A few days later on the maid's day off, Rose is spending a welcome hour or two mistress of her own kitchen. She is making the family meal without Elena's diminutive, bustling form whisking away dirty dishes to wash or hovering attentively in case the Señora should want her to dice or slice anything.

Rose turns the dial on the radio to Radio Ciudad which broadcast to the English-speaking community of Mexico City. It has chat shows and phone-ins and quizzes and, of course the news. It is one of Rose's lifelines to "normality". The presenter has that deep, resonant voice with the familiar cadences so typical of American broadcasters. Rose is half listening to the prattle of a phone-in programme as she prepares the filling for stuffed pork chops, frying the onions, celery and mushrooms and adding the breadcrumbs to the mixture. It is St. Valentine's day and many of the calls are about such topics as "my first love". The programme is laced with musical dedications to lovers ... it is mostly women who phone in. Rose turns her attention to the cream cheese chocolate cake she is preparing as a special treat for the children. It is their favourite. She uses some of her precious American chocolate which is like gold-dust to find here and almost as expensive. The radio drones on as she pours the batter into the heart shaped tin she found in the *mercado* last week and puts it into the fridge to set. The DJ is back following a commercial break and the familiar "Radio Ciudad" jingle.

"Hello Delia and how are you today, and where are you phoning us from?"

"Hi Dan. I'm just fine thanks. I'm calling from Condesa where I live with my darlin' husband and my four children."

"Bully for you," mutters Rose.

"What do you want to talk about today Delia?"

"Well Dan, I was just wondering, seeing as it is Valentine's day and all, why anyone would want to name the day of love after such a terrible massacre? I just don't understand what the connection is?"

The presenter is nonplussed. Rose holds her breath, chocolate-covered spoon poised mid-air between the mixing bowl and her lips, waiting for his response. There is none. It must say something in the Radio Presenters' Manual: "On no account, no matter how stupid the caller, must you pass any judgement or make any negative comment."

"So, Delia from Condesa," continues Dan, disguising the smirk in his voice, "did you get anything for Valentine's day?"

"Oh, no, Dan, 'fraid not. Ya see, I suffer from unrequired love, but don't tell my husband!"

Rose winces at the malapropism and Delia's girlish giggles.

"Well, I sure won't tell him, but I'm afraid maybe you just have, Delia honey. This is Radio Ciudad, the number one station of the nation, back after these messages."

There follows a further series of commercials. Rose can pick out one for a popular drink and one for the washing powder she uses. Her Spanish is what she calls "kitchen Spanish" and for now it is all she needs to get by. She would have to remember Delia from Condesa to tell Peter and the girls at dinner. It would make for an amusing anecdote and these days she didn't have many funny stories to tell. Rose is bored. She needs some diversion in her life, some excitement. She thinks about Delia, so smug in her lovely home with her children and a husband she is contemplating cheating on. Is it because, like Rose, she has too much time on her hands?

Rose begins to visit Mrs Puchetti more often until it has practically become a daily ritual. At 4 pm she takes her place opposite the old lady on the patio. Mrs Puchetti is always on her own at this time. Sam is at work, Natasha is either engaged in one of her many activities or having her siesta, and the boys are taking part in some extracurricular sports game depending on the season. The two women talk over tea and the famous almond biscuits. Sometimes Rose brings the remains of something Elena has made for dessert that lunchtime, sometimes they drive to the little tearoom in Polanco and have tea there. Over the next few weeks the two women develop a close, comfortable relationship. To Mrs Puchetti, Rose is like the daughter she has always longed for. Her daughter-in-law, Natasha, for all her beauty and intelligence, is not a warm person and, unlike Rose, does not share Mrs Puchetti's quirky sense of humour. And to Rose this kind, elderly lady helps to dull the ache of homesickness for her friends in New York and her own mother and sisters in London.

New Neighbours

Mrs Puchetti has invited the Jacob family over for Sunday lunch in the garden.

"My son and daughter-in-law will be here, and it is time you all met, seeing as the girls are becoming so chummy with my two louts of grandsons!"

Upon arrival the children soon settled into a game of volleyball, Esther with Giovanni and Dilly against Gregorio and Arturo and Gail. The grown-ups sit in the shade of the patio with their drinks and some snacks and dips. The boys' parents make a striking pair, both tall and slim. Sam's longish hair is greying at the temples and Rose is struck by the almost violet colour of his eyes and his long dark lashes. Natasha has long, deep auburn hair which falls into natural ringlets, and extraordinary green eyes. She wears a green blouse and white pedal pushers and jewellery which complements her outfit, tasteful but not ostentatious. Rose admires her poise and elegance but senses a certain aloofness in her, in contrast to her husband who has an easy manner and dry sense of humour which appeals to her. She can see that he takes after his mother.

They watch as the children play and the small garden lizards, disturbed from their siesta in the sun by the noise of the children, dart in and out of the ivy. After some general chit chat about moving, new surroundings, the altitude, the neighbourhood, Rose and Natasha and Sam and Peter begin two separate conversations. Mrs Puchetti soon dozes off in her chair, drunk with the heat and the gentle burble of chatter around her. Sam and Peter are talking sport, which baseball team they support and where the best golf course is. The two women discuss the children, Natasha giving Rose helpful advice about doctors, markets, and the best department store from which she could purchase the girls' school uniform at a fraction of the price charged by Hidalgo's, the outlet recommended by the school. Thus passes an idyllic Sunday afternoon. By the time the Jacobs leave, Rose feels that, at last, she is beginning to put down roots in her new life.

A few weeks later, a large moving van pulls up outside the house next door to the Jacobs'. Up until now it had been empty. Throughout the day there is a parade of moving men taking furniture and boxes into the house. The air rings out with the sound of a woman's voice, a sweet voice with a southern accent.

"Jamie! Y'all be careful with that lampshade! Take that box of stuff and put it in your room. Heather darlin', please get rid of that gum 'fore it eats a hole in your gut and hang up your clothes. At least your room has a closet."

A man's voice, same southern twang, but deep and resonant, floats over the wall from the alleyway between the two houses.

"Sandy, honey, where do you want this box?"

A dog yelps.

"Oh, sorry fella. Hey one of you kids put this poor mutt out in the garden, he's over excited and keeps gettin' in the way!"

A young girl, about Esther's age, emerges from the back kitchen door. She wears braces and glasses, and the sun glances off both of these as she catches hold of a small white terrier and ties him to a gatepost by a tree at the back of the house.

"Good boy Harley. I'll bring you some water, 'kay?"

The dog wags its tail happily and then whimpers as the girl disappears with a bang of the screen door.

"Sand, Sandy!" the man's voice again. "Have you seen my briefcase? I have to get back to the office. Oh. Here it is, I've got it!" he shouts. "Bye y'all. See you tonight."

Rose watches all this coming and going from her bedroom balcony. Now the man, tall, with a crew-cut and a giant frame, steps out into the midday heat. His hands are huge, like two hams, Rose muses. One carries a leather briefcase whilst the other unlocks the door of a green and white convertible. He starts the engine and drives off up the road and around the corner, headed for the Paseo de la Reforma which would take him into town.

At 2.30 Peter and the girls arrive home. The school day is over for the girls, but, after a meal and a siesta, Peter will be returning to work. He will leave the Chevy with Rose in case she has some errands to run with the children, and she will pick him up from the office later on. It is the usual family meal with an exchange of news about the day's happenings, and funny little anecdotes that this or that one has to relate.

"Mrs Gonzales, my English teacher got so cross with Davy Jones today. When she gets angry her face goes all purple and these big veins stand out in her neck and she screams!"

Dilly grimaces and holds her breath in an attempt to make her face go purple.

"Eat your salad, Dilly."

"It tastes of floor cleaner."

"That's just the purifying tablet. It won't harm you. Eat it up!"

"Yukky."

Gail waits for a pause in the conversation. Dilly consumes a lettuce leaf, screwing up her face and pinching her nose as if about to dive under water.

"Señor Maldonado speaks so fast, Mom," Gail says, "and he expects me to understand everything he is saying. How can he expect me to be fluent in Spanish? I've only been in the stupid school for a term, and he puts me straight in with the Intermediates. It's not fair! Everyone laughed at me today because I answered "Si sēnor" when he asked me something. I thought he asked if I was listening, but Katie told me he asked if I was dreaming! I hate him!"

"You'll get used to him and your other teachers and I bet you become fluent in Spanish within six months," her mother said.

"I think Señor Maldonado is funny," pipes up Esther, unhelpfully. Gail glares at her. "But Miss Joseph is horrible. She gave Pamela a conduct card just because she didn't do her geography homework ... so mean. Pammie was in tears all through recess. And she gave us a project to do. She cut up bits of paper and wrote a country on each one of them, folded them up and then put them in a box which she passed around the class. Guess which country I got?" she paused here for dramatic effect. All eyes were on her. "Italy!!"

"Good choice!" remarked Peter. "Italy's a great country to study with all its history and culture."

"We'll have to find some material for you to get your information," said Rose. "The Encyclopedia will be helpful but you can't just copy great chunks out of that, not unless you want your project to be really boring. You'll need to go to the school library and find other books that might help you."

Esther thought for a moment.

"I know! Instead of drawing a map I can make a map using plasticine! I can put in the mountains and the main rivers with tin foil and make flags to stick in showing which areas produce which crops!"

"That's a really good idea!" interjected Peter. "And I have a bit of chipboard in the garage you can use to build it on."

"Actually," Gail interrupted her father, "you know Esther, Spanish is one of the Romance languages which means its roots are in Rome where they used to speak Latin and, actually, Italian and Spanish are very similar."

Gail's "actuallies" were beginning to irritate Esther. She said it in such a superior tone of voice, like Esther was stupid or something.

"I mean your project could have a section about the language too," she finished helpfully.

Rose nodded her approval at this suggestion.

"Yes! And you know what you might think about doing Esther? You could maybe do an interview with Mrs Puchetti! She is Italian and could tell you so much about what it was like growing up there."

Esther thought about this for a moment.

"Do you think she would mind me bothering her?"

"Not at all! I'm sure she would love to sit down with you for a chat. Let me to speak to her and arrange a time for you to go over there. Maybe start by writing down what questions to ask her, then you can make notes as you go along."

Finally, Rose tells them about their new neighbours. The girls are so pleased to have an English-speaking family right next door with children their ages. They can't wait to finish their meal and go upstairs to their rooms which overlook the alleyway between the two houses and catch a glimpse of the new occupants.

Rose rings the little bell by her place setting to summon Elena to clear the table. It still doesn't sit right with her to have a servant doing things for her and she has everyone pass their plates down the table for her to pile up to facilitate this task for the maid.

The following week Esther keeps her appointment with Mrs Puchetti. She is rather shy about going to the Puchetti home without her sisters, but she likes Mrs Puchetti who is in her usual place on the patio and immediately puts her at ease.

"Sit, sit!" she says and motions Esther to the chair opposite her with the table between them. There is a big pitcher of freshly made lemonade and a dish with a doily piled high with some pastries and chocolate chip cookies. She pours out two glasses of lemonade and motions to the dish saying: "Help yourself! A good journalist needs nourishment!"

Esther helps herself to an éclair, taking care not to squidge too much cream out of the sides. Luckily there are pretty linen napkins to deal with any faux pas in the eating department. She rolls her eyes with pleasure and Mrs Puchetti beams at her. She has a soft spot for this little girl. She has watched all the children at play and has noticed that Esther is shy but is also the one that is empathic, sharing and being kind to the other children. She loves watching her in unguarded moments, as she dances under the trees, her skinny long arms swaying above her head or enters a make-believe world in character.

"So, I understand you have an assignment about Italy. I can tell you plenty! Fire away!" Mrs Puchetti adjusts a cushion in the small of her back and leans in to listen.

Having disposed of the éclair and a cookie, Esther takes out her notepad and pencil and clearing her throat, starts with her first question. An hour later she returns home with a notepad full of Mrs Puchetti's life and a paper bag full of chocolate chip cookies.

Within a week Heather and Jamie are enrolled into the British School and Esther and Heather have become inseparable. They are in the same class, they do their homework together and play in each other's houses or go over to Mrs Puchetti's garden for a less exclusive game of tag or hide-and-seek or Red Rover with their siblings and Giovanni, Gregorio and Arturo. Esther loves going over to Heather's.

Her mother, Sandy, makes frequent trips to the border. She has a small business as a buyer of Mexican artefacts and curios for a firm of interior designers in Dallas. On the first Friday of every month Sandy piles the trunk of their convertible high with boxes of statuettes, bark paintings, wrought iron lamp stands and candle holders and drives overnight to avoid the blistering heat of the day to the border town of McAllen. More often than not she shares the driving and the cost of gas with friends or acquaintances who need to go to the border to renew their residence permits or want to do some shopping stateside. Once in town, she hands the consignment over to Tony or Chris of MEXART Inc., and then books herself into a motel. Here she strips off her travel clothes and heads straight for a long, refreshing shower. Then she lies on one of the two double beds listening to the television and the gentle hum of the air conditioner, the cool air caressing her skin. More often than not she falls into a deep sleep and awakes refreshed in the early afternoon, ready for a bite to eat and then ... shopping!

As a result of these monthly trips, Heather's kitchen is a cornucopia of goodies. Esther can't believe her eyes when Heather casually opens one of the kitchen cabinets to reveal rows of Oreo cookies, Aunt Jemima Pancake Mix, Tootsie Rolls, Betty Crocker Brownie Mix, Almond Joys and Jiffy popcorn. Esther loves going to Heather's for a snack. It is like being back home in New York. The girls spend hours together playing jacks on the cool blue and white tiled floor in Esther's hallway, or making up little plays with their Barbie dolls in Heather's bedroom which is always so tidy. Esther now has to share her room with Dilly and they have to make their own beds and clean the room once a week.

"Elena is not your servant," Rose would say. "You make a mess; you tidy it up."

Heather does not have the same responsibilities. There is a place for everything in her room, and no younger sister to come along and mess it up. There are shelves for her books, a closet for all her clothes and a window seat that lifts and can store all her games. There is an old chest, like a treasure chest, at the foot of her four-poster bed and the bed itself has a canopy that matches the immaculate bedspread of rosebuds and cherries. Esther loves the way Heather's pillow sits at the head of her bed, all puffed up with a dent down the middle in which her soft toys (a donkey and a teddy) nestle. She starts to do the same with her pillow. Her side of the room is separated from Dilly's by a tall bookcase. Esther's side looks like a hotel room waiting for occupation, Dilly's side looks like Hurricane Donna has been through it and then come back for more. Esther lines her books up neatly on her desk and makes two signs out of card: "THINK" and "PLAN AHEAD", this last with the "D" squeezed in at the end indicating that the author has failed to do just that. Esther thinks this is very clever and witty. The fact that she understands this joke makes her feel suddenly very grown up. She nails an empty tissue box to the wall beside her bed and keeps a small flashlight and little treasures in it. She has to share a long dressing table with her sister with three big drawers on each side. Esther's side is dusted and polished with her brush and jewellery case neatly arranged. Dilly's side remains piled high with dirty socks, bits of string, rocks and half chewed Crayola crayons. There is a massive mirror over the dressing table. Esther peers into this with wonder at the image it throws back at her. Who is this gawky, freckled, curly haired freak? Why can't she have flowy princess-type hair and a flawless complexion? She spends hours applying talcum powder to her face to block out the freckles and to cover her short crop of curls, she puts one of her mother's black half-slips on her head and tosses it over her shoulder whilst she plays out some story or other. When listening to her records she picks up the hairbrush and uses it as a microphone as she mimes the words.

It is mid-June. The Jacob family have been in Mexico for almost a whole year. The end of term is approaching, and the children are in high spirits as they spill out of school. They stroll up the road to the bus stop and flop onto the grass under a palm tree, resting their heads on their satchels and gazing at the blue sky through the palm leaves. Dilly is on look-out for the bus.

"Whaddya wanna do this afternoon?" Jamie addresses the jumble of bodies around him.

"Tag," offers Dilly, executing a perfect cartwheel.

"No let's make brownies and play Barbies," says Heather.

"Yes!" agrees Esther.

"Aw. Come on you two, let's all do something together," demands Gail. "I know. We'll make a picnic with real lemonade and sit in Mrs Puchetti's garden. We can make up a play and Cha Cha can be in it!"

There is general assent and then the jumbled mass start up as one, collecting satchels and cast off blazers and ties as Dilly yells: "BUS!"

The bus travels the few blocks down the Paseo de la Reforma, past the Dairy Queen and the big white houses with their orange tiled rooftops and tall black wrought iron fences, past the jacaranda trees and the bougainvillea-clad balconies. The children crowd off the bus and head down the side street that leads into Avenida de los Picos. There is a house on this street, one of the more modern, rectangular-shaped houses with large picture windows, all built on one storey. This is the home of "Charlie", a very large Alsatian dog. As they approach the house the children taunt him.

"CHAAAAARLIEEEE!" they sing. As soon as he hears them approaching, he tears down the driveway and barks and snarls at them through the railings of the gate. The first few times this happens, the children sensibly walk on the other side of the road. But they soon realise that Charlie's gate is always padlocked shut. They become less and less fearful and more emboldened, woofing at the dog as they pass and sending him into a frenzy. Now as they start down the road feeling the euphoria of the first taste of the summer vacation ahead, they sing out: "CHARLIE! Oh CHARLIE!"

They hear the familiar scrabbling as Charlie leaps up and runs to the gate, but this time, to their horror, the gate is wide open. Charlie is in a froth of anger. At long last revenge is in his grasp. He tears out of the gate after the children.

"Run!" shrieks Gail.

"Mommy!" cries Esther.

Gail grabs Dilly's hand and Esther grabs her satchel, and they all belt up the road, across the street and into the Jacobs' drive, slamming the gate behind them and laughing hysterically. Charlie sniffs at the gate and barks gruffly a few more times before heading back to his bowl of water in the cool shade of his garden. That is the last time they would tease him! After changing out of their uniforms and with a little picnic of bread rolls and cheese and fruit and a flask of lemonade, the children check that Charlie is out of sight and emerge from their houses walking down the road to call on Greg and Giovanni and Arturo. They while away the afternoon under the parasol of Mrs Puchetti's generous trees. Later on, the adults will join them for a barbecue and card game. This has become a Friday night ritual. Mrs Puchetti insists that the venue should be her house.

"I so enjoy the company," she explains to Sam, "but I am getting too old to last the whole evening. At least here they will understand if I take my leave early and no one will be disturbed. Anyway, the children do love playing all together in the garden."

So, it is agreed that Rose and Peter would bring dips and nibbles, Sandy and Ed would bring salads, whilst Sam and Natasha would supply the chicken pieces, succulent steaks, hamburgers, hot dogs and of course some Puchetti's ice cream for dessert.

This evening, Esther arrives earlier than the rest. She is keen to show Mrs Puchetti her project which her teacher had returned to her with an A+. They sit at the patio table and Esther sets out the plasticine map of Italy and the booklet she has made divided into sections for History, Geography, Language and Culture and Mrs Puchetti's Story, with a photograph of the old lady pasted onto the front page, and a flag showing where she was from inserted onto her map.

"My, my," Mrs Puchetti beams. "It's a fine project! I love the map and the way you have presented all this information."

She pores over the map and leafs through the project, every now and then chuckling softly to herself.

"You have done very well Esther. Very well done my dear!"

Esther pulls herself up in her seat. She has a tingly feeling at the back of her neck and her stomach does a somersault. She is not used to such praise for her academic efforts. Mrs Puchetti continues, "and because you have worked so hard, I have a little prize for you."

Esther is also unaccustomed to receiving prizes. That was more her sisters' department. So, her eyes widen as Mrs Puchetti puts a small gift box wrapped in pretty paper and tied with a silk bow onto the table.

"Open it my dear."

Esther undoes the bow and is careful not to tear the paper. She opens the box and inside on a plush velvet cushion, is a silver bracelet with a charm of Italy hanging from it.

"Oh!" she exclaims with delight. "This is so pretty! I love it! Thank you so much!"

"Here let me help you put it on." Esther goes round to Mrs Puchetti's chair and holds out her wrist as Mrs Puchetti secures the clasp for her. She holds it aloft admiring it and then embraces the old lady, kissing her on both cheeks.

"I am so glad you like it. I hope you will think of me when you wear it."

"I will!" enthused Esther. "And every time something wonderful happens in my life I will add a charm to it!"

By seven o'clock everyone has arrived. Esther shows off her bracelet which is admired by one and all. It is a beautiful evening after a stifling day. The sky is pink with feathery, silver clouds. It looks like a painting stretched on a vast canvas. The garden is freshly mown and the fragrance from the cut grass mingling with the pungent smell of the barbecue is intoxicating. The children run amongst the trees and Cha Cha barks joyously at all the attention she is receiving. Arturo helps Sam build the fire and watches the others at play. Sam sends him off to the kitchen to collect the platter of chicken thighs and steaks. When he returns with them Sam ruffles the boy's hair and says: "Ok Arturito. *Ya, vaya con los otros a jugar.* Go play with the others."

And he is off with a whoop to join in the game. The adults sit around a large picnic table on the patio. They sip wine or beer from glasses the colour of amethyst or turquoise that Natasha had bought the previous week straight from the glass factory. She had watched as the glass blower fed the furnace and then withdraw a long hollow pipe from the embers. Almost as if by magic, by a process of blowing into and turning the pipe, the substance at the end began to take shape and metamorphose into a beautiful goblet or vase or a flower. He made little glass animals and a set of six tumblers. He made a glass flower the colour of amber, pinching out the petals before the glass cooled and set. He handed this to Natasha with a gallant flourish. So impressed was she by the creative process and the breath-taking results of his craft, Natasha decided to fill the trunk of the car with full sets of tumblers, glasses, pitchers, three vases and a present for Mrs Puchetti … a delicate little glass spaniel.

The families get on very well together. Rose and Sandy have become close in spite of the fact that they are really from quite different worlds. Sandy is entrenched in all those Southern values which are rather alien to Rose, though she did admire Sandy's entrepreneurial spirit, running her own business. In that respect she was ahead of her time. However, they have enough in common, the children, their move from the States, and a similar sense of humour. It doesn't take them long to start sharing confidences and offering mutual support, both practical and emotional in this foreign land.

"I don't know, Rose," Sandy had said one morning over a cup of coffee. She had come over to borrow Rose's iron as hers had succumbed to years of use, finally giving up the ghost in a most spectacular manner, fusing all the lights in the house. That had been two hours ago. She stretches out on the sun lounger on the Jacobs' patio, hitching the hem of her skirt to her thighs to top up her tan. She sips her coffee daintily and continues: "I just sometimes feel that Ed looks right through me. He comes home, grumbles about his day at the office, grumbles about the heat, grabs a beer from the fridge, slumps in his chair and that's it for the evening. I tell you I could just sometimes scream from boredom. If it wasn't for our Friday nights, I'd go stir crazy."

Rose tuts sympathetically.

Sandy takes another sip and having reached the coffee grounds, tips them into the shrubbery next to her, sending a lizard darting up the wall into the security of the ivy.

"It's good for the poinsettia. Anyway, where was I? Oh yes. Ed and me. I mean look at me Rose."

Rose looks at her. She has an immaculate complexion without a line on it. Her blonde hair is in an attractive page boy, straight and glossy, whereas Rose's dark curls are at present drawn back into a ponytail to keep them from corkscrewing all over the place in the morning's humidity.

"I mean, I'm only 42. I want to see a bit of life before I shrivel up into an old prune."

Rose likes Sandy very much, but cannot see for the life of her what had attracted her to Ed. He is a gentle giant of a man with a rather course sense of humour, and he is not what Rose would consider at all sexy. She can't see where the chemistry between Ed and Sandy is.

"You must have fallen in love with him at some point," offers Rose.

"Well ... sure!"

Sandy sits up and slides her sunglasses onto her head, squinting in the glare of the morning sun.

"I was working as a receptionist at Hernandez Furnishings in Dallas where he was chief buyer. He was much older than me, you know, a man of the world. Up 'til then all the men I knew were just silly boys into the three Bs – baseball, beer and boobs, and little else. He was so suave by comparison. He could afford a nice meal in a real restaurant with linen cloths on the tables. He was so self-possessed, in control of his life, you know what I mean?"

Rose nods.

"I thought to myself, this guy knows where he's going, and he'll look after me. So, we married and before we knew it, we had two kids and a dog and a mortgage. And he's been a good husband and a caring father. He's just, I don't know, he's just sort of set in his ways."

Sandy speaks apologetically. She doesn't want to appear to be disloyal to Ed. She loves him really; she just isn't in love with him anymore.

Rose gives this some thought as she freshens their coffee cups.

"Maybe," she chooses her words carefully, "maybe you are just too romantic, Sandy. 'In love' doesn't last. It can't, or we would all be going around looking like zombies. But caring for someone, sharing their life, respecting them and feeling secure with them, that is a love that endures, don't you think?"

"But he never shows me he loves me. He used to do all sorts of little things and say all sorts of cute things to me. Nowadays I'm lucky if he remembers my name! Still, I suppose it could be a lot worse, couldn't it?"

Rose smiles at her friend and replies: "Sure could. At least Ed is loyal and faithful."

"Yeah. Like a great big ol' Saint Bernard."

That had been several weeks ago. Now on Mrs Puchetti's patio the adults are deep into their card game. The light on the patio wall has been turned on. There is the distant sound of a basketball bouncing off the walls as Giovanni, Greg and Jamie pass it to each other and through the hoop hanging above the garage door. The girls are playing ping pong in the garage, which is big enough to accommodate two cars, a ping pong table, a large chest freezer and a dart board.

"Come on Sammy boy. Don't keep us in suspenders!" semi-jokes Ed with a slight edge to his voice.

Natasha sighs in exasperation: "Get on with it honey."

"There you go! A run of four and two groups of three!" Sam sits back triumphant whilst everyone else moans and throws in their hands.

"Another beer anyone? How about you Ed, Peter?" Sam opens two bottles and hands one to Ed. Peter declines.

"I'll go make some coffee," says Natasha and disappears into the kitchen.

"Not for me," declares Mrs Puchetti. "I'm off to my bed. Good night all!"

Sam helps her out of her chair, handing her her walking stick.

"G'night ma, sleep well," he says and plants a kiss on her forehead. She strokes his cheek. He is still her little boy. He and the boys are her only real blood ties now, for it is unlikely that she would ever see her only surviving sister again.

Sam's good night kiss tells his mother she does not have to be afraid; she is not alone. He would always be there to look after her. As she disappears up the staircase to her bed Sam re-joins the party, sitting back down heavily on the canvas chair.

"You look tired, Sam," observes Sandy. "You all right?"

Sam looks up.

"Yes, yes, I'm fine ... just overdoing it a bit, you know, working all day and then trying to keep up with this place in my spare time."

He makes a sweeping gesture which takes in the house and garden. Natasha has insisted that they need extra room now the boys are older, so Sam has drawn up plans for an extension and called in contractors and builders to get the job done as quickly as possible, if that is at all possible in Mexico City.

"I hate all the waiting around for the plasterer and the plumber and the bricklayer who say they will come at a certain hour on a certain day and then don't turn up! And work is sheer hell right now. We've moved offices and my files are all over the place. The office itself is great, overlooking Chapultepec Park, but it is much bigger than my other office. It just looks so bare, and I need something to dampen the level of noise. Every time the phone rings it sounds like an air raid siren! I need to buy a big rug and maybe some books to fill all the shelves and get myself a few pictures to hang on the walls ... Ah! Coffee!"

Natasha carries a tray with a percolator, a small pitcher of milk and a sugar bowl and six ceramic mugs, each with a different flower painted onto it. She had made these herself at a pottery class the year before.

Rose admires Natasha. She is a bit of an enigma. It isn't that she is unfriendly, but there is an aloofness about her and a directness that sometimes borders on rudeness. She is cross with Sam this evening for giving Lupe the evening off when they were expecting company.

"For Chrissake!" he had exploded earlier on, "all we have to do is make a few damn cups of coffee and throw some steaks onto the barbecue and we'll be using paper plates."

This was just the touch paper that ignited the fireworks of a much wider argument which encompassed everything from the frustration with the building work to their non-existent sex life. To the outside world they were a couple ideally matched with their striking looks and their comfortable lifestyle. They worked well as a family unit, but they tended to have their own interests and their own schedules. These days they rarely even sat down for family meals. Natasha and Sam often communicated through the notes pinned to the kitchen bulletin board or written on the family organiser calendar:

Friday: Natasha meeting 7 pm – no dinner

Wednesday: 4 pm boys to dentist – Sam

Saturday: 2 pm Greg and Giovanni swimming at the club – Nat

Natasha said what she felt when she felt it, like a child, almost brutally honest. She was tired and wanted to go to bed and she had no qualms about saying so to her guests, adding that they were welcome to stay as long as they wished. She left them to their coffee.

Feeling slightly uncomfortable and let down after what had been a pleasant evening, Rose raises her eyebrows at Sandy as if to say, "who rattled her cage?". She gulps down her coffee trying not to look at Sam who shrugs apologetically and says cheerfully: "Who's for ice cream!"

Rose feels awkward and a bit sorry for him. Shortly afterwards the party breaks up and everyone goes home.

The following Wednesday Mrs Puchetti and Rose assume their usual places on the patio.

"You pour the tea dear " offers Mrs Puchetti , "that teapot is so heavy I'm always afraid of dropping it!". She calls Arturo to bring out the plate of biscuits which Lupe had baked fresh that morning. Arturo carries the plate back very carefully from the kitchen and places it on the table.

"*Gracias, cariño.*"

Arturo goes back into the dining room to sit with Dilly. They get on very well. They sit side by side at the big mahogany table and do some colouring. Dilly has brought along some shiny sequins and they paste these onto their drawings. They chat all the while in a mixture of Spanish and English.

"No, Dilly, *así no*, not this way, *pon lo aquí*, here put it here!"

"Ok, *ya Arturito, déjame*, I'll do it myself!"

Mrs Puchetti has a slice of lemon in her tea, Rose adds milk from the delicate little milk jug.

They are talking about Natasha.

"She has always had everything her own way. She has my Sam wrapped round her little finger. He works too hard and then spends every spare minute working on the house and, before we had Pedro, chauffeuring the boys here, there, everywhere! And still she complains that this is not done or that is not fixed. She is the youngest in her family and I think she was very spoiled by her rich parents. And my Sammy is too good natured, he does not know how to say no. He is a saint like his dear father!"

Here she crosses herself and looks piously heavenward from where Rafael without doubt is watching over her.

Rose wonders how the Puchettis all manage to live together under the same roof. There are obviously tensions in the air and Mrs Puchetti herself can't be the easiest mother-in-law to live with.

"The latest is that she wants to go, by herself, to Acapulco for a whole week in September so she can do some writing and Sam, like a fool has said yes! What, I ask you, is the point of a marriage if you do not do things together. Mr Puchetti and I were inseparable until the day he was taken from me."

Again, she crosses herself and embellishes the sentiment with a little sniff into her handkerchief.

Rose reaches out and strokes Mrs Puchetti's arm, realising that she becomes emotional whenever she mentions her late husband.

"Things are a bit different these days. Lots of women go out to work. Look at Sandy with her own little business. We have more independence. It doesn't mean that Natasha doesn't love Sam, she just doesn't feel they have to live in each other's pockets."

Almost on cue the gates open and the car glides down the driveway with Pedro at the wheel and Natasha at the back returning triumphant from her shopping expedition. She scatters several bags around her as she collapses into one of the patio chairs.

"Whew! It's hot and I'm all shopped out."

Rose recognises the names of one or two fashionable stores on the bags.

"What did you get?

"Oh, a new costume and a sun hat and two new paperbacks and a beach robe. Just a few odds and ends for Acapulco."

Mrs Puchetti does not disguise the sour look on her face and purses her lips in disapproval.

"I'm going to see if the children want some biscuits," she says and picks up her walking stick and the plate of almond biscuits and goes into the cool darkness of the living room, tapping her stick loudly with each step on the flagstones to emphasise her pent-up anger with her daughter-in-law.

Natasha fails to sense her mother-in-law's disapproval. Perhaps after all these years she is immune to it and can shrug it off.

"I'm so thrilled," she bubbles, turning to Rose. "Five days, five full days on my own. I've bought a notebook for each day and I intend to fill each one cover to cover."

"What will you write about?"

"Oh, I don't know yet, but I'm sure the words will just flow out of me as soon as I get to my little room in the hotel."

Rose doesn't feel the same ease that she feels when talking to Sandy. Natasha is more reserved, but they are able to discuss books, films, theatre, politics and art. It's funny. She needs both of these women to complement the different facets of her makeup. With Sandy she can happily discuss marriage, kids, Jackie Kennedy's latest outfit and the best way to remove unwanted hair.

"Honey, you just have to yank it out with wax!" Sandy would say.

With Natasha she can talk about Civil Rights, the Cuban missile crisis and the socio-economic situation in Mexico where the massive gulf between rich and poor is all too evident, even on their front doorstep, even in their own homes.

The two women smile as Dilly and Arturo emerge into the garden and they watch them at play, making up elaborate stories in the generous shade of the trees.

"I think Dilly will be fluent in Spanish before the other two," muses Rose. "Arturo is a great influence and is doing better than the school at teaching her."

"He's a great kid alright. He has his mother's good nature and his father's good sense and he's more resourceful than either of my boys."

"I'm so glad the children have settled and made friends. What was it like for you when you first came here? I'm still finding my feet, but I must admit that without all the household chores and cooking to do, I'm finding myself at a loose end sometimes."

Natasha studied Rose. She didn't know many English people and Rose and Peter were quite different to her usual friends. They had this understated, quirky sense of humour and had had experiences she had only read about in books. Whilst she had been enjoying a carefree youth in Boston with parties to go to and boyfriends at her feet, Rose and Peter were in the middle of the war, with bombs falling on their city and both of them in the services. She couldn't imagine what it was like to cower in an air raid shelter, carry a gas mask all the time, not eat a banana! This pretty Englishwoman, with her lovely accent and wealth of experience was like a breath of fresh air to Natasha.

"Well, when I first came here after Sam and I got married I had the babies to look after and I was pretty isolated, not knowing anyone and stuck in the house most of the time. The only socialising we did was with Sam's clients and friends and I really missed my girlfriends and my Mom especially. Life here is so formal so getting to know other people and make friends was hard work. Funnily enough, what saved me from going mad was the British Institute. I met other women there attending lectures or films. And there is a local Arts centre which runs workshops for expats like us. They do all sorts there like pottery and creative writing. Oh, and there's a little bookshop in Polanco, near the teashop. It specialises in selling English books and they have monthly lectures which are very interesting. I'm going next Thursday evening if you're interested. I think it's about the history of the Aztecs and their influence on modern day Mexican arts and culture."

"Now that is an offer I can't refuse!" smiled Rose. "If you're sure you don't mind me tagging along, I'll look forward to it!"

Later on that evening Sam is walking Cha Cha up Avenida de los Picos from the little park at the end of the road. Sandy is struggling ahead of him carrying two bags of groceries.

"Hey, Sandy! Hold on!" Sam and Cha Cha jog across the road. "Let me help you with those."

"Thanks," she says, as Sam takes the bags and gives her the dog's leash.

"These are heavy. What you been buying?"

"Oh just a few groceries. Ed needed the car this evening. I didn't realise how much I needed from the store. I got a bit carried away and forgot that I actually had to walk back with it all."

Sam liked Sandy. He liked the easy way about her, her openness. She was uncomplicated, vivacious, and life for her seemed to be a celebration. He could not imagine her feeling depressed. The first time they had met her, he and Nat had joked about her. They had referred to her as an airhead, a southern belle with that awful drawl and that blonde hair. He felt guilty now that he knew her better ... She was quite sweet and natural, really.

"How's the cave?" she asks.

Sam looked puzzled.

"The cave?"

"You know, your big cave of an office. You sorted it all out yet?"

"Oh! That cave! God what an ordeal that's been. Do you know it took me a whole week to find some drawings for a client? Everything is in such a mess. I've more or less sorted out all my files now, I just need to find a few bits and pieces to make it look nice, but other than that I'm installed."

They arrive at Sandy's gate and exchange dog for parcels.

"Thanks for your help, Sam, I appreciate it."

"My pleasure Ma'am," he fakes a Southern accent and bows, mockingly, in an old-fashioned way. He holds the gate for her and watches her go down the drive to her front door.

"See you Friday," he calls after her. She doesn't turn around, struggling with the parcels and the key to open the door.

"Yep. See ya then," she calls back.

And then hearing the door close, he shuts the gate.

"Come on Cha Cha. Chow time!"

Sam

Sam sits in his new office poring over some drawings for alterations for a house in San Ángel. It is one of those beautiful colonial properties which, like most houses in this exclusive part of the city, is hidden from the tree-lined road by a high stone wall topped with multicoloured shards of glass. The exterior is built in a honey-coloured stone and some of the windows are arched shaped, like in a church. Indeed, one window is of stained glass. It depicts a fanciful version of the arrival of the explorer Cortés as he and his entourage ride between the two snow-capped volcanoes, Popocatepetl and Iztaccíhuatl into the valley of Mexico City. The scene is dwarfed by an enormous sun coming up between the two volcanoes, its golden rays fanning out above and behind them and offering a golden carpet between them on which Cortés is about to step as he leads his expedition to glory. Sam likes this house. The owners had been careful to retain all the original features and were anxious that Sam's adjustments (an extension to the kitchen and a laundry room) were in keeping with the general design and feel of the house.

It is cool in the office. A fan drones in the corner. Outside the rise and fall of the cicadas and the distant hum of the city traffic can be heard. A hummingbird, metallic-blue and ruby-red, hovers over the hibiscus in a window box on the balcony. A lazy fly settles onto an empty coffee cup on Sam's desk, next to a calendar clock and a photograph of his family in an elaborate silver frame. Sam is standing at his drawing board immersed in the challenge of fitting in all the elements of the utility room he is creating. The intercom on the desk buzzes. He's in no hurry to answer it, finishing off the elliptical shape depicting the space for a washbasin before leaning over to press the button.

"Yes Beth?" he says.

His secretary, sitting no more than a few feet from him on the other side of his office door, squawking through the intercom announces: "I have a Sandra Cooper out here asking to see you. She doesn't have an appointment. Shall I send her in?"

Sam doesn't recognise the name, but then he has never been very good with names and it could be a client.

"Send her in, but tell her I've got half an hour here before I head for home."

The door flies open and Sandy breezes in, smiling and carrying a large cardboard box. The effect of her entrance is that of a cannonball firing through Sam's stomach practically knocking him off his chair. In that split second it is as if someone had reached into the core of his being and pulled him inside out.

"Well hello Sand-RA," he teases, recovering himself. How formal! I never would have guessed. And what's with the surname?"

"It's my maiden name," she explains carrying the box across the room and setting it on a leather chesterfield sofa. "I use it for my business. I like to keep it totally separate from Ed's business activities, it's less complicated tax wise and anyway it's my baby! Look I'm sorry to interrupt your work but I was just passing on my way back from an auction. I bought a job lot and look what it had in it! I thought you might like them for your office."

She removes two small Aztec figurines from their wrapping of newspaper and unwraps a beautiful bark painting in a gold leaf frame.

"The bark painting is unusual, don't you think?"

Sam looks at the painting. Most bark paintings are painted in bright, almost fluorescent colours. This one is more sedate, green foliage on a light, bark background, perfect for his office wall.

Sam fumbles around for words.

"They're very nice, thank you! What do I ...?" he reaches in his back pocket for his wallet.

"Oh please!" exclaims Sandy, putting her hand on his arm. "It's my pleasure. I love finding things for friends, and it honestly didn't cost much. Consider it an office-warming present."

Sam smiles at her and tries to say in a nonchalant manner: "Well. I think that deserves a coffee. How about it? I know a nice little coffee shop around the corner."

"I would love that," smiles Sandy. Sam thought she made even a cup of coffee sound light and enjoyable and ... fun!

"I'll just phone home and tell them I'll be a bit late."

Sam tries to analyse what had happened to him when Sandy walked into his office. It had been such a physical reaction, he reeled from it for days afterwards going over the scene again and again. How she had touched his arm, sending an electric current through him, how she had smiled as she chatted and looked at him when he spoke, and caught her hair back into its bun as she looked at the menu in the café they went to. He tried to reason with himself.

"She's just a friend, a good neighbour" was like a mantra going through his head whenever he felt butterflies in his stomach, or his heart pounded faster giving him a lightheaded feeling. He tried to convince himself that Sandy's visit had been nothing more than a neighbourly gesture, but suddenly he had such a yearning in him. There was this yawning chasm in his very being that screamed out to be fulfilled.

"What on earth is the matter with you, Sam?"

Natasha and Sam are standing in the shell of their new extension. Sam has rolled out the plans onto a wallpapering table and appears to be immersed in them although his mind is in a different place.

"Huh?" he jumps.

"I've been standing here asking you what you want for supper. You're on a different planet these days. Are you okay?"

"Oh, yes. Yes!" he says, turning to give her his full attention.

"It's just that I'm stopping off at the market on the way to my lecture and I wondered if you wanted anything special."

"Right well, I don't know, honey, you decide. I'm happy with whatever you and the kids want."

"Okay. I'll be back around six. Lupe is taking Arturo to Polanco for a picnic with her uncle this afternoon, so anything you need you'll have to get for yourselves."

"Fine, see you later hon'."

Sam looks after her as she strolls to the car. She looks so nice with her dark auburn hair piled on top of her head and those satiny green pedal pushers which show off her trim figure. He had loved her for a long, long time, but somehow, somewhere along the road they had lost sight of each other. After Greg and Giovanni were born, he had work, she had the babies and by the time he came home she was too tired to talk, never mind thinking about lovemaking. He kept telling himself things would get better and was as devoted as ever, any surplus energy went into work, the house and the children. When the children were older and less demanding of her energy and time, Natasha threw herself into study, taking several extra-mural courses at the University and attending workshops at the British Institute.

"It's me time," she would say, "a chance to get away from all these domestic demands and do something just for me."

And Sam had agreed, had encouraged her, was proud of her. He looks after her now as she gets into the car and reverses out of the drive giving him a wave. He raises his hand, but she doesn't look back to catch the gesture. He looks at his hand, suspended in mid-air, and he is suddenly overwhelmed by the kind of sadness one feels when saying goodbye to someone who is a part of you. Was that what was happening? Was he saying goodbye to that part of his wife who was his mate, his confidante, his lover? Had their relationship been reduced to schedules and the demands of family life with little if any room to rediscover the lover in each other? Their exchanges were often peppered with barbed words, sarcastic comments or exasperated looks. Mrs Puchetti would sometimes intervene with a cross "*Ya basta!*" accompanied by a loud tap of her walking stick. It distressed her when they spoke to each other like this, and she couldn't remember the last time she saw them hold hands or embrace each other.

Just as years ago, at a party, Natasha's dazzling smile has suffused him with a sudden boundless joy, now her almost dismissive wave from the car filled him with a longing he could no longer ignore.

Later that afternoon he phones Sandy to thank her again for the Aztec figurines and the bark painting. Over the months they had spoken on the phone countless times to make arrangements for taking kids to parties, to issue invitations for evenings out to the theatre or cinema or sorting out the school run, but suddenly the sound of her voice aroused him. He realised that he wanted to see her again.

"I might be able to find some other stuff for you if you like. I've seen some lovely rugs, one or two of those would certainly make your office look more inviting and absorb the sound too."

"Sounds good to me," Sam says, trying to ignore his pounding heart and sound cool and composed.

"Fine. I'll see what I can find at Wednesday's auction and drop them in on my way home. Does that suit you?"

"If you're sure it's not out of your way?"

"No, not at all. See you Wednesday."

Had she sounded seductive or just friendly? The night before at their usual card game, neither one of them had spoken about her visit to his office. Had she kept quiet, as he had, in order to keep it their secret?

Tea and Tlaloc

Natasha is headed for a lecture on Tlaloc, the Aztec Rain God. Tlaloc is in the news. The monolith of this deity had slept soundly for centuries in a dried-up stream in the small village of Coatlinchan, thirty miles from the city, but in a few months they would be bringing him to Mexico City to stand at the entrance to the new Museum of Anthropology. Natasha loved going to these monthly lectures at the little bookshop in Polanco. The subjects varied from talks on the Arts and history to the lives of famous people. Last month's lecture was about the life of Eleanor Roosevelt whose autobiography had been displayed prominently in the window of the bookshop. Today it was the turn of Tlaloc, the city's latest celebrity and the shop window is full of books about the Aztecs. Natasha spotted Rose beckoning to her from the second row of seats and waved back, pleased that she was there. She made her way to the seat next to her apologising for disturbing those who were already seated at the end of the row.

"Looks like I just made it in time," she said, shrugging off her jacket and removing her glasses from her handbag before placing it at her feet.

Rose handed her a programme.

"I thought I was going to be late. I had to take Peter back to work, but the traffic was terrible around the Ángel. I think a bus broke down or something. But here I am, ready for the Aztecs!"

She held up a book with Tlaloc on the cover.

"I'm already doing my homework!"

The buzz of chatter died down as a dapper, elderly man with a good head of grey hair and a beard and moustache to match it, stepped up to the podium. The lights were dimmed, and the slide show began. Rose felt a frisson of excitement. She suddenly realised how much she was missing going to cultural events and, like a plant denied water, she soaked up every word this man said. In New York she had gone into Manhattan with her friends once or twice a week to a gallery or a lunchtime concert whilst the children were at school. Although many of Rose's friends had had careers before marrying, really only a couple of them, both divorcees, held down full-time jobs now. Helen was a teacher and Dena a psychologist. She admired them tremendously as they struggled to make a living and raise their children with little if any support from ex-husbands or extended family. The rest, like her, were bringing up young families and homemaking. Here in Mexico she felt isolated and, other than attending Spanish lessons once a week, she did not venture very far from home. On the way out after the lecture, Rose swept up all the brochures and prospectuses displayed on a small table by the reception desk and put them in her handbag. She and Natasha decided to stop off at the little tearoom for tea and cakes before heading home to the demands of their families.

"I love this place!" she said.

Rose and Natasha sat at a corner table which looked on to the small park.

"It reminds me of a place in London which we used to go to for afternoon tea. It's right opposite the Royal Academy in Piccadilly and, before the War, my sisters and I loved nothing better than going to an exhibit with our Mum and then having a cream tea at Richoux. This place has the same feel about it and the cakes are just as yummy!"

Her eyes sparkled as she sank her teeth into a pastry.

Natasha laughed.

"You look just like one of the kids set loose in a candy store!"

They talked about the lecture and pored over Rose's brochures, deciding which other lectures and activities they could go to, and classes Rose might enjoy.

"You know," Rose sat back in her seat looking relaxed and happy. "For the first time I feel like I could make a go of it here. Thanks so much for being my guide, Natasha. Honestly, I don't think I could have taken another week of deciding which silver needed polishing, planning meals and ferrying the girls to ballet or to visit school friends. If it hadn't been for your mother-in-law putting up with me yabbering on about all my worries and how homesick I am, I would have gone stir crazy! Now at least I can plan in a few activities just for me each week."

"Glad to be of service ma'am !" Natasha said in a southern drawl, pitching it to sound like Sandy. It was the first time Rose saw a different side of Natasha. She actually did have a sense of humour ... albeit a rather cruel one.

Sam felt like an adolescent getting ready for his first girl/boy party. He felt almost sick as he checked the clock on his desk for the fifth time in as many minutes: Wednesday 11th July, 5.05 pm.

He swivelled back round on his architect's high chair to face the drawing board. Sandy breezed in a minute later, a triumphant look on her face and two beautiful woven rugs draped over each arm. She did a twirl as if showing off a new dress and sashayed towards him like a catwalk model at a fashion show. Stopping before him she said: "Zee latest in interior design. Does Monsieur like zem?"

Sam reached out a hand to touch the rug she held out to him, but instead he drew her towards him and kissed her, just gently on the lips, tentatively, like two butterflies brushing against each other. Sam felt years of yearning falling away as the rugs dropped to the floor and he felt her arms around him, her fingers caressing the back of his neck. He was kissing her now with more assurance, his tongue exploring hers, his hands exploring her face, her arms. Suddenly all of his senses were alive to the touch of her, the smell of her, the sound of her voice as she murmured his name. He had forgotten how powerful a kiss could be.

Sam was in love.

They began to meet regularly every Wednesday at first, but then whenever they could. It was scary and it was exhilarating. Sam did not feel guilty. He surprised himself with how guilt-free he was feeling. He was delirious with the joy of it all. He almost wanted to share it with Natasha, this momentous thing that had happened to him. As his partner, as his friend, surely, she would rejoice with him. To absolve any feelings of guilt he did have, he became hypercritical of Natasha. He would take an almost sadistic pleasure in picking an argument with her. He could then feel perfectly justified in walking out and meeting up with Sandy at a coffee shop, in a restaurant, or going on a long drive into the countryside where they would park in a secluded spot and spend the late afternoon making love. Sandy represented all that was understanding and loving and carefree whilst Natasha represented all the demands and responsibilities in his life.

Sandy, meanwhile, hugged her secret to her like a mother with her new-born child. Waves of delight washed over her unexpectedly whenever she thought of Sam and she would catch herself smiling foolishly or daydreaming for minutes on end. She would have liked to confide in Rose. She was so overwhelmed by what had happened that she felt as if she would burst if she didn't tell someone. But this was Mexico City in the early sixties and even though women in the US were beginning to find their voices and take the pill, women's lib had not reached the English-speaking colony here, and an affair was still considered quite scandalous.

Sam had never felt like this about any woman before. He loved Sandy's receptiveness, her playfulness, her soft girlishness, so different from the practical, brilliant Natasha with her hard edges and brutal directness. Sam began to question why he had married a woman who was so unlike himself. He had admired all of those qualities in her that he lacked, but as the years passed, those very differences became their battleground. Natasha was provocative and dynamic, and she made Sam feel that he should always be on the move, always involved in some intellectual pursuit or other when all he really wanted to do was lie in a hammock and read the sports pages or watch a baseball game on the box in the middle of the afternoon. With Sandy he felt at ease with himself, at one with himself, without any pretence or compromise.

The weeks slipped by.

The families still got together on Friday nights. For Sandy and Sam these evenings were a sweet torture. There was so much inner turmoil, they were sure that the others could almost hear it emanating from them. One Friday, Sam and Sandy took a casual stroll around the garden.

"I want to go away with you. I want to spend a whole night with you. Can you get away?"

"I think I could, after all I do spend nights away when I drive down to McAllen. I'm sure I can fit in an urgent consignment for Tony and Chris!"

"And I can invent a meeting with clients in Cuernavaca followed by wining and dining them and a field trip to look at properties the next day. We can go to Acapulco and stay at the Elcano."

"Sounds perfect, I can't wait."

"Nat's away for a few days next week so we'll have time then to get together, maybe a day trip and dinner in San Ángel? We can plan our big escape then."

They rounded the house and stopped near Pedro's vegetable garden. Locked in each other's arms they kissed and touched each other, only breaking it off when Cha Cha came bounding up to them with a happy bark and a wagging tail.

A few minutes later Pedro entered the kitchen with a wicker basket of vegetables over his arm, freshly picked. He could not hide from Lupe what he had witnessed, shockingly, beyond the shrubbery that hid him from the lovers. Lupe was at the kitchen table peeling some peaches for a fruit salad.

"What's the matter? Are you ill? You don't look right *mi amor*."

She stood up and reached out to feel his forehead. He grabbed her hand and led her out of the kitchen into the garage.

"I've just seen el Señor kissing that woman!"

"What? Which woman? Señora Jacob?" Lupe held her face in her hands staring at Pedro in disbelief.

"No not her, the blond one. They were all over each other. They were just a few centimetres from me! I was sure they could hear my heart pounding. I didn't know what to do, cough loudly as if I was approaching them and hadn't seen anything or stay crouched over my aubergines like a statue. I chose the statue option. I thought they would never leave. Thanks to God Cha Cha started barking and brought them to their senses! This is bad Lupe. If the Señora finds out it could have serious implications not just for the family, but for us too! What if they divorce? What if she leaves him? *Dios mío* what a mess!"

"*Cálmate cariño*," Lupe soothed. "There's nothing we can do so there's no use fretting and hopefully the affair will die a death. I knew that woman was trouble. She thinks she's Marilyn Monroe! You know what these gringos are like ... in and out of each other's beds. It wouldn't surprise me if they're all at it. The main thing is that no one finds out, but I don't know how I can face either of them, carrying such a dreadful secret. They need to be more careful!! For goodness' sake it could have been Arturo who caught them at it!

Lupe returned to her kitchen to finish the fruit salad. She made Arturo take it out to the patio and kept herself to herself for the rest of the evening, waiting until everyone had gone home and the Señores had retired to bed before clearing the dishes and resetting the table for breakfast.

Adolescence

Esther was now 14. She had had her first period, her first bra (a Maidenform size 30 AAA) and was looking forward to her first kiss, with whoever that may be. Esther and Heather would spend the two breaks in the school day walking around the schoolhouse, arms linked, talking about boys. Esther was in love with Zac Henderson who had those wholesome good looks and chiselled features seen on the covers of romance novels.

"I just love the way he says 'Esther' and the way his hair goes at the back, and the bit that flops over his forehead. I just love everything about him."

"I know." agreed Heather, giving her friend's arm a squeeze. "It's the same with me and Mark. And he gets all the latest Beatles records even before Radio Ciudad does, cos his Dad's in the business."

They rounded the back of the schoolhouse and watched some boys playing "chicken" with a compass. This was strictly forbidden, but the teachers rarely checked the back of the house on their break duty, but that is where the smoking and illicit games of spin the bottle and chicken went on and if they caught the kids at it, they would have to put them in detention which meant they too would have to stay after school! Best not to look.

Esther and Heather had been invited to a party on Saturday. They had so much to talk about – what to wear, what to do with their hair, where to get ready. They decided to get ready at Esther's house. Heather wanted to wear her new hipster mini skirt. She knew that Ed would not allow her out of the house in it, so it would be better to go from Esther's with Peter who didn't seem to be so strict with his daughters' attire.

Mr Geppy rang the school bell and the children filed back to class. It was Latin for Esther and Heather. Esther was afraid of Mr Howell. He expected her to know what a principal part was and how to conjugate a verb, and if she stammered or hesitated or got it wrong, he would slam his textbook on his desk, sending a zillion particles of dust into the shaft of morning sunlight that streamed through the window onto the bent heads of her classmates.

"Heaven help the sailors on a night like this!" He would hiss, incandescent with rage. All of her teachers were characters in one way or another in this little outpost of England. Esther reckoned they were all either running away from an unhappy relationship, or they were wanted in connection with some heinous crime, or they were alcoholics. They all knew for certain that Mrs Gomez, the maths teacher, was divorced, drank too much (even in school) and was having an affair with the headmaster. They knew this because Mimi Bowden had seen her come out of his office one day crying.

Esher's favourite teacher was Mr Thornbull. He taught French. He was a young, fresh-faced Englishman, all shining teeth and glasses. He must have just finished University and Esther reckoned he had come to Mexico for an adventure. He was full of energy and very funny. He had the habit of playing with the cord of the venetian blinds as he strode up and down at the front of the class reciting verbs.

"*Je suis, tu es. il est, elle est!*"

Suddenly his foot would somehow become entangled in the cord and the blind would come crashing down with a loud metallic clatter as Mr Thornbull hopped about trying to extricate himself. His face would go purple as he snapped his fingers and pointed at each of the laughing faces.

"Shu-up! Shu-up! You! Shu-up. Silence!" This last said in French to show that he meant business.

One stifling day, the classroom was so hot, the atmosphere of sweaty bodies and chalk dust so overpowering, that several pupils were nodding off over their French textbook. Mr Thornbull was sitting at his desk. It was the last lesson on a Friday and he had set enough written work for Upper School 3 so that he needn't stir himself unduly. He surveyed the sea of bent heads as he leant back in his chair, as usual twisting the cord from the venetian blind around his fingers. Suddenly, as he teetered on the back legs of the chair, there was a loud crack and one of the chair legs went right through the floorboard. Mr Thornbull went over backwards, bringing the blind crashing down on top of him. Esther looked up from her exercise book to see a puff of dust and the soles of Mr Thornbull's shoes hovering over his desk like two puppets in a puppet show. Mr Thornbull disentangled himself from the venetian blind.

"Shu-up! Shu-up!" he shouted.

He took his gold-rimmed glasses off and polished them with his tie, stuck them back on the bridge of his nose and carried on as if nothing had happened, as if the crater beneath his desk and the pieces of twisted aluminium were nothing at all to do with him. He strode between the rows of desks, with his hands clasped behind his back, occasionally stopping to correct a mistake.

"No, no, no Marsha, not 'le' it's 'la', how many times do you have to be told it's feminine!"

Or thwack the back of one of the boys' heads: "wake up Brooks, what do you think this is, the Ritz!"

However, the most popular member of staff, for the girls at any rate, was Mr McCarthy. He could teach anything, Latin, Algebra, English, he was so clever and he looked like Paul McCartney and he drove a red MG. He was really "sharp". Unfortunately for Esther, Rose had arranged for Mr Mac (as his students referred to him) to come into her house – right inside her house! – for extra coaching in Latin and Algebra. Esther hated it. She had to sit right next to him for a full hour every Tuesday afternoon, getting things wrong, her ignorance undiluted by the antics of her classmates. To make matters worse, Rose would bring him tea and biscuits halfway through the lessons. She had to watch as he did such a mortal thing as eat and drink.

The upside of all this was that Esther was consequently the envy of all the girls in her class.

"He had two chocolate chip and one almond biscuit, and he told Mum he lived in San Ángel"

Esther's friends listened attentively to her feedback from the previous day's tuition.

"He took his tie off, you know, and undid his collar button. He has a few hairs just here," Esther said, pointing to her upper chest.

"Ugh," said Sophie, "I hate hairy men.'

"Oh, I think he's just dreamy," Roxy swooned back into the cool grass under "The Tree". This was the largest tree in the school grounds and the main source of shade in the heat of the Mexican sun. The Tree stood tall and strong in spite of the wounds to its bark in the form of hearts and initials and arrows. The rest of that break was taken up with further discussion about the party. Only three days to go till Saturday!

Heather came over to Esther's at about four o'clock on Saturday afternoon. That would give them a good four hours to get ready. They made out a schedule and wrote it on Dilly's chalkboard.

4.00-500 pm hair

5.00-6.00 pm nails

6.00-7.00 pm make-up

7.00-7.30 pm get dressed!

Esther put 20 rollers of different sizes in Heather's straight hair to make it wavy. Then, in order to straighten out her friend's natural curls, Heather wrapped Esther's wet hair around her head, securing it with a hair net. They then both sat under the bonnets of their respective hairdryers which made so much noise that they were unable to chat and had to resort to the back copies of *Seventeen* magazine that Gail's friend would send her occasionally from the States. Every now and then they would nudge each other with their foot and point to something on the page they were reading. After half an hour, Heather would wrap Esther's hair the other way round her head and the drying would continue. Once dry, Esther would then don a woolly cap to keep her hair from kinking.

As they painted each other's toenails, (they were only allowed colourless nail polish. They had to be 15 before coloured nail polish was permitted, for some strange reason) they chatted and listened to the music on Radio Ciudad.

"My Mom's gone funny," said Heather.

"Mmm?" encouraged Esther.

"She's sort of silly and giggly all the time, but then she can suddenly get into a temper and she cries real easy these days. I never know what mood she'll be in from one minute to the next."

"Maybe it's the change," Esther nodded wisely, "they go funny with it."

Heather, not quite sure what "the change" was, ignored this and continued …

"And Dad is like this light bulb with this crazy moth just dancin' and bangin' up against it all the time. And they've had some big fights."

"What about?" Esther was intrigued. Her parents only ever behaved as if they were always in love. Every time he came home her Dad and her Mum would embrace and spend an hour before supper having a drink and talking about their respective days. They didn't argue. They were a united front, never saying a definite "yes" or "no" to requests from their daughters, but "we'll see", and the final verdict was only ever handed down after joint consultation.

"Oh, stupid things, you know. Like Dad watching too much baseball or leaving his socks under the bed, you know, really silly things."

"They're just going through a phase. It's probably nothing," soothed Esther, secretly hoping her parents never went through a phase like that.

At 7.45 pm they were almost ready, and the chatter had reached an almost hysterical pitch. Peter called up to them: "Est! Heather! Ed's here!"

"What?" they called out in unison. "But Dad, I thought *you* were going to take us."

"No, sweetie, Mum needed the car so Ed said he would take you. I'll pick you up, though, at about eleven. Okay?"

There was a flurry of activity. A few minutes later the girls came downstairs, Heather looking demure in Esther's grey school uniform skirt over her mini hipster. She would whip it off just as soon as they got to the party.

Natasha breathed a sigh of relief as she entered the sanctuary of her hotel room. At last! The day had seemed interminable and had gone through more twists and turns than the Labyrinth of the Minotaur. There were moments when she thought she would never find the exit. Natasha was a Bostonian, brought up and educated amongst the elite of that city. She had met Sam on a family holiday one Christmas, at a party in Acapulco. Sam was there agreeing some plans for a hotel with the landowner and the local bureaucrats. It was one of his first jobs as a newly qualified architect, and it helped him secure a position with a well-respected firm of architects in Mexico City. She thought of him now as she flopped onto the bed, in that very hotel, staring at the ceiling of her luxury room. She could hear the shushing of the sea, the buzz of the cicadas and the occasional cooing of a dove. The balcony door was open and the soft early evening breeze, bearing the scent of jasmine and honeysuckle and geranium, made the net curtains billow out into her room like two white sails. She closed her eyes and contemplated the events of the day.

She had taken a taxi to the airport. The driver was friendly and chatty. He kept turning around every time he wanted to say something to Natasha who gripped the hand strap above the window and tried not to look ahead of her. This was not unlike a white-knuckle ride at the fun fair. Sure enough, as the taxi rounded a *glorieta*, it collided with a bus. Natasha recalled the sights and sounds and smells around her. The floral mosaic around the fountain with its peeing cherubs and spitting Gods. It was a big fountain, and the rushing of the water almost masked the angry swearing of the two drivers as they exchanged insults and nearly came to blows. It all ended in a bear hug, an *abrazo*, to seal an agreement not to involve insurance companies or the police. Natasha's driver handed over several hundred pesos to pay for the damaged rear brake light on the bus. The taxi, however, was not in such good shape, and could not be moved. It was beginning to cause a traffic jam all the way up each of the four roads that fed into the *glorieta*. Natasha gathered her bags together as her driver hailed the driver of a *cocodrillo* – a taxi with green spines painted along it making it look like a crocodile as it slithered through the morning traffic. Natasha tried to ignore the honking of horns, the shaking fists and the cat calls of other drivers.

"*Oiga, guapa. Ven conmigo. Yo te puedo conducir al cielo, si quieres!*"

She did not, however, want to be driven to heaven, just the airport. The driver of the *cocodrillo* managed to get her there with just a few minutes to spare before her flight was called. Once on the plane she sat next to a nun who did nothing but pray and cross herself for the entire flight. She would raise her voice every time the plane hit a bit of turbulence adding an extra notch onto Natasha's anxiety level.

"You won't believe what happened next!" she would say to anyone who would listen over the next six months, at her lectures, in the doctor's waiting room, at parties. "Well. I got into this taxi from the airport to my hotel. We were driving along the main mountain road. As we rounded a bend two children, no older than eight or nine, ran into the road and slung two live iguanas in front of the taxi, forcing us to stop. They had tied their tails together and suspended them at the window urging me to buy them. Suddenly these two men, these bandits, came out of nowhere, held the driver at gunpoint and took all of his money and my handbag! I tell you, I was so scared. I thought that was the end, that I would never see the kids again, that they would rape me then kill me and my body would never be found. They threw the driver's keys into a ravine and then they were gone. My poor taxi driver was so upset. Poor man. He had lost all of his takings for the day and I wasn't going to be able to pay him my fare either. We hitched a lift in a Coca Cola truck into Acapulco. The truck driver was so nice. He gave us each a Coke and delivered the driver to the police station and then me straight to my hotel. That must have been a first. A near hysterical guest, sunburnt, dusty and penniless, pitching up at their luxury entrance in a Coca Cola truck."

Natasha opened her eyes and sighed. She would have to phone Sam to arrange for money to be sent to the local bank and no doubt the police would want to question her, although for all she knew one of the bandits was probably related to the chief of police and the case would go no further.

"Damn!" she said out loud. "So much for getting away from it all."

She swung her legs off the bed and stood up to inspect her room. This was her space, her hideaway for five whole days. She ran her hand over the white embroidered bedspread and smiled with satisfaction at the polished wooden floor with two small throw rugs on either side of her bed, and a gorgeous, thick hand-woven rug with pictures of birds and deer around the edges in turquoise and mustard in the living area of the room. The furniture was heavy colonial and there was an exquisite lace cloth runner on top of the dresser and a green leather inlay on the solid desk. This was situated in front of the balcony with its view of the citrus gardens leading down to the sea. She could take in the sweep of the entire bay from the French windows. Here is where she would write, uninterrupted by the demands of her sons, Sam's sawing and hammering, her mother-in-law's complaints, Arturo's whistling and Lupe's soap operas. She listened again and smiled. All she could hear was the rustling of the ivy as the geckos darted in and out of the sunshine and the booming and shushing of the Pacific Ocean as its waves rose and fell onto the white, white sand.

Meanwhile back in the city Sam and Sandy had their own plans.

"Hon'! I'm taking the car, see y'all later!" Sandy called from the hallway.

Ed lumbered to his feet from his armchair and stood, his large bulk framed by the living room door.

"Where ya goin'?"

His forehead was furrowed, and his head bent to one side. He thought he might have missed some piece of information that his wife had given him. These days he tended to select what he listened to what with all the kids' chitter chatter and Sandy's domestic arrangements. He found that by and large he could get away with an "Uh Huh!" to satisfy most requirements of a conversation.

"I told you hon'. Don't you ever really listen to me?"

He shrugged, looking sheepish. Sandy sighed in exasperation and then as if talking to a child.

"I'm going to be at an antiques fair all day and then I'm meeting up with some dealers for dinner. I'll be back at about 11.30. Okay ?"

"Okay sugar lump. Have fun," he called over his shoulder as he returned to the third inning of the Yankees versus the Dodgers.

His armchair received his bulk with a groaning of springs as he raised his beer bottle to his lips with one hand and scratched his crotch with the other. He sighed with the sheer pleasure of having a whole ballgame to himself without interruption.

Sandy shut the door behind her and let herself out the front gate. She started the car and drove up the road. She turned right and right again down the road which ran parallel with Avenida de los Picos. Sam was waiting for her on the corner. She stopped and he got in. They giggled like two naughty children. With Natasha away it was like a holiday for them. At least they didn't both have to make up lies about where they were going or what they were doing. Sandy just had to come up with some plausible reason for being out of the house for a few hours. She knew Ed was too plain lazy to imagine infidelity on his wife's part and would never think to check up on her, verifying times and venues. Of course, Sandy never named the names of people she was supposedly going out with or to visit. She would just say in a vague way with a dismissive gesture – "oh, just a bunch of us are going to a movie" – or she would name a "friend" he had never met, who only existed in his wife's world, a friend from the hairdressers, a friend from the PTA or some such.

Today they drove out of the city to Xochimilco, a magical place where you could hire a small boat festooned with fresh flowers to punt down the river. The waterways were banked by dense forest and you were accompanied on your journey by electric-blue dragon flies, butterflies of every hue, exotic birdsong and the distant sound of a mariachi band playing. Sam had gone to great trouble to pack a picnic hamper and as they drifted down the river, they ate cold chicken with potato salad and French bread and butter. They drank a crisp, cold white wine, clinking their wine goblets together.

"*Salúd, dinero y amor y tiempo para gozarlas,*" they toasted, to each other's health, wealth and love, and time to enjoy them all. Then as they drifted down the waterway, they lay back watching the canopy of trees and the blue sky passing above them as they kissed and fed each other almond chocolate and plump juicy grapes.

Later they drove to San Ángel where they were unlikely to bump into any of their friends or acquaintances. They went for a meal at an inn. They drank more champagne and danced on the patio overlooking the beautiful gardens and then went up to the room Sam had booked and spent the rest of the evening in each other's arms. Before they left the inn, Sam booked them in for the Friday night. If asked he could make up some story about a night out with the boys, getting drunk and falling into a comatose state on Jorge's sofa. Sandy just had to mention an extra trip to McAllen to deliver some artefacts to MEXART.

On the way home they listened to Pat Boone singing "April Love" on the car radio. Sam sang the whole song, his voice deep and resonant. They parked around the corner and agreed a late morning meet up the next day for a walk in the park. Sam got out of the car to walk home. By the time Sandy opened her gate and let herself into her house, Ed was asleep in front of the blank TV screen and Sandy was totally in love with Samuel Angelino Lorenzo Puchetti.

Esther was also in love, with Zac Henderson. He had kissed her to the strains of "Blue Velvet" coming from Bobby Steven's Motorola record player at the party on Saturday night. Even though their lips had failed to make contact, he caught her chin, and she got the side of his nose, it was her first kiss, and she would never, ever forget it. The party had been in full swing. Esther and her friends danced frenetically to "The Twist", "The Mashed Potato" and "The Loco-motion", and sang all the lyrics to "Crying in the Rain", "The Wha-Watusi and "Speedy Gonzales" before someone turned down the lights and put on the "slowies" and the dance floor was left to those in search of adventure.

The following weeks at school brought a flurry of exchanged glances and, in class, scribbled notes scrunched up by the numerous hands through which they had to pass before Zac, in the back row, made contact with Esther in the front. She would feel a prod in her lower spine from Roxy's ruler and she knew there was a message from her beloved.

She waited for the teacher to turn to the blackboard then hold out her left hand behind her back to receive the message. She would stare steadily in front of her, pen poised in her right hand as if she was the most dedicated of pupils. In fact, she hardly noticed what work was being done in class during those weeks after the party. She was a full-time student of love.

> *Every day I see you*
> *Sitting in the room.*
> *Then my heart is pounding*
> *Hear how it goes boom.*
> *Esther is my flower,*
> *Rosy like a bloom*

Heather and Esther sat under The Tree. Esther read the poem out loud to Heather for the hundredth time and squealed with delight.

"Look at that. Look how the first letter of each line spells out my name! Isn't he just the neatest, sharpest boy!"

She swoons back clutching the poem to her bosom.

Heather was jealous. Things had not worked out so well with Mark Thomson. He had got off with that bitch Lesley halfway through the party. All of Heather's friends had crowded into Bobby Steven's bathroom to commiserate with Heather and say how dreadful that Lesley was – what a scheming bitch. She knew that Heather loved Mark.

"Her mother would have a cow if she could see how fast Lesley is," proclaimed Roxy, applying a pink blush to her lips and touching up her eyeshadow in the bathroom mirror.

She smiled and admired her braces which had become something of a status symbol with her peer group.

"Yeah, and it's not the first time she's stolen someone's boyfriend. Bitch," said Maisie Drew, vying with Roxy for the mirror as she backcombed her hair.

"Bitch!" they all echoed.

The toilet, tastefully partitioned off from the rest of the bathroom by a tiled wall, flushed, and Heather emerged red-eyed and blotchy-faced. It was almost worth losing Mark for all this nice attention she was getting from all the girls.

By Monday she was fine and, having made suitably impressed noises about Zac's poem to Esther asked: "What do you think about George Marlow? Don't you think he has the dreamiest eyes?"

Esther followed Heather's gaze to where George was playing chicken with some other kid from the year below.

"Mmm. He's okay. He has a nice smile. Tell you what, I'll get Zac to get him to come with us skating on Saturday. Okay?"

Over the last year or so, Mexico City had acquired a bowling alley, several hamburger joints and an ice-skating rink. It was as if a bit of America had come to Esther's doorstep. Years later she would wonder at how small minded she had been. When she was older, a sight, a smell, a sound would fill her with the most tremendous nostalgia for Mexico and she would resent the American influence she could see spoiling the culture, the very landscape of places she was to visit as an adult. But here and now, in 1964, the ice-skating rink was the place to hang out, show off and flirt on a Saturday afternoon.

"Remember Esther. You stick with the others, no wandering off on your own, even to the bathroom. You understand?"

Rose and Peter were always anxious when one of the children went out unchaperoned.

"Aw, Ma, you sound just like Peter Rabbit's mother warning him away from farmer McGregor's garden."

"Don't forget about the Eccleston girl," Rose said, looking stern.

Esther and her sisters had heard this story many times. The Eccelston girl had gone to the cinema with her friends. She sat at the end of the row eating popcorn. Suddenly the woman sitting behind her tapped her on the shoulder.

"Excuse me young lady, but I'm feeling a bit faint, would you be a dear and help me to the ladies?" the lady had said.

When Rose told the story, she would pause here to make sure the girls were all listening. Then she would start again: "The rest room was just there on the left side of the cinema and the lady sounded American and seemed harmless enough. Seeing as the movie had just begun, the Eccleston girl decided not to disturb her friends. She took the woman into the Ladies."

Rose would again pause for effect here, taking a sip of tea or lifting the hem of her shirt waister dress to rub off some non-existent mark. The three girls would watch her, waiting for the next bit.

"Once inside the Ladies this woman covered the Eccleston girl's nose and mouth with a hanky soaked in chloroform. Another woman came in and she said: 'Hurry up. The chloroform won't last too long'. Between them the two women carried the girl to an awaiting car explaining her state away as having fainted to the usher and doorman.

"And do you know?" Rose would say. "That was the last anyone ever saw of her."

"Wasn't there a ransom or anything?" Gail would ask.

"No. She wasn't kidnapped for money. She was probably shipped to another country and sold into the white slave trade."

The "white slave trade" was like a neon sign which lit up in Esther's head whenever she became separated from her friends on one of their outings. She would be truly terrified for her life if she ever found herself abandoned by them.

Today the giggling, swaggering, noisy group of adolescents skated for two hours with a half-hour break for hot chocolate and hot dogs covered in a batter. George had ploughed into Heather so many times, thus registering his interest. Her heartbreak with Mark was soon forgotten as Heather turned her attention to George. Esther was happy because now she and Heather could compare notes on an equal footing.

Natasha had tried to get hold of Sam all evening. Mrs Puchetti said he was at some kind of meeting, but was rather vague and did not know when he would be home. She tried one last time at eleven o'clock, but he was still not back.

"Pretty late meeting," she said to herself as she stared into the bathroom mirror to put on her night-time moisturiser. It was one of those mirrors with two side panels. You could move the panels to see yourself in profile and from behind. Natasha looked at her profile. She was not displeased with what she saw although she could see a few streaks of grey threaded through her hair. The beginning of the end. She was tempted to pull them out, but had heard that if you did that, nine more would grow in their place. Better leave well enough alone.

She turned off the bathroom light. Moonlight cast a shaft of light across her desk and the wooden floor. It was hot. She would leave the balcony doors open. As she lay in bed watching the rise and fall of the net curtains in the light breeze, her thoughts turned again to Sam. It bothered her that he was not there with the boys whilst she was away, even if his mother and Lupe and Pedro were on hand, it wasn't the same as one of their parents. She sighed heavily as she admitted to herself that she and Sam were not getting on. He was so tetchy these days and would explode at the slightest thing, always blaming her for whatever had triggered him off. Was he ill? He had had a medical check-up a few months before and he said he was fine "in tip top condition," he had boasted. She wondered if he was under some kind of pressure at work, although he had not mentioned anything out of the ordinary and seemed to be enjoying his latest project on the house in San Ángel.

Suddenly Natasha salt bolt upright in her bed.

"He's having an affair. Oh my God. He must be having an affair."

And with just that thought, Natasha's world suddenly became twisted and distorted. She tried to reason with herself. She had no proof, no actual evidence of an affair. She, Natasha was the guilty one for not trusting him, for being suspicious for sewing the first little poisonous seed that would spread and infest their whole relationship. She had been listening to too many of Lupe's soap operas. However, the worm of suspicion had burrowed into her thoughts and she spent a troubled night making up scenarios in which Sam might be conducting his affair.

"Hi, hon'. I got your message. What's doin'?"

It was the morning after her sleepless night. He sounded normal, chirpy. Why was he so chirpy?

"I phoned till eleven last night," she said, her heart pounding, but she managed to steady her voice, which wanted to scream out: "Where the hell were you last night!"

"Yes, I know. Sorry, Nat. I had to have a drink with some clients. They had come all the way from Fort Worth specially to see me and wanted to seal the deal with dinner and a drink at Fernando's bar."

"Who was there?" She tried to make the question sound light.

"Oh, you know, me and Rob and the two clients, that's all," he said, not liking lying to Natasha. He felt bad, but did not realise he would be facing the Spanish Inquisition when he phoned her. "So, what's up?"

Nat told him about her ordeal the day before. He tutted and made soothing, sympathetic noises. He agreed to wire her some money immediately.

"What are you up to today?" she asked.

"Nothing much. You know, this and that. I have to take Greg and Giovanni to basketball practice so will probably end up at Texas Jim's for a burger with them."

"Good, they'll like that."

She could feel her heartrate slow and her breathing became more even. He sounded so perfectly normal. How could she doubt him??

They talked about his project and her writing. She didn't admit to the still pristine pages of her notebooks.

"But Friday night I might go and play some cards with Jose Antonio and Jorge after dinner," he said.

This was safe. Natasha had little to do with his male friends, they were part of his life before he had met her and continued to be throughout the years of their marriage. His buddies, his "playmates" as Natasha scornfully called them. Everything he said was plausible and at first, after she had hung up, Natasha comforted herself with his explanations.

"I'm stupid," she thought. "How could I believe that of Sam?"

She tried to shrug off this feeling she had, but it kept gnawing at her until it totally consumed her thoughts. Her notepads remained blank, her books unread, the swimming costume still in its original wrapping. Natasha decided to cut short her stay in Acapulco and go home a day or so early. These feelings would go away once she was back in familiar surroundings, on home ground, and could talk to Sam face to face.

Sam sounded tired and irritable when Natasha phoned him to let him know that she would be home on the Friday instead of Saturday. When asked, he said that he had had a bad day. There were some alterations he had to do to some plans, and then when he got home, Arturo had left the garden hose on and the water had run down the drive into the garage and under the wood pile. Of course, in reality he was annoyed that he would have to call off the night away with Sandy. He would have to call her to let her know. He could already hear the disappointment in her voice, he knew how much this one lousy night meant to her.

"Damn Natasha," he thought, his reaction like that of a child whose mother had spoiled his fun by making him come in from playing and do his homework.

Natasha arrived home looking far from rested. She had dark circles under her eyes and seemed ill at ease, edgy. She tried to behave normally, but something within her was driving her to do things she would never have dreamt of a week ago. Whilst Sam was at work, she took his clothes out of the wash hamper and inspected his shirts for lipstick or a hair or the smell of perfume. She riffled through his chest of drawers in the bedroom and his desk drawers in the study looking for check stubs, letters, receipts, a note, a phone number, anything that would be a clue to his infidelity. After each frantic search she would feel better – no evidence equalled no affair. But then the nagging doubts would start again, eating her up, consuming her. She almost willed some evidence to turn up so she could feel justifiably outraged, upset, betrayed, jealous, anything – anything was better than feeling like this. Concrete evidence would be the poison required to kill off this seed of doubt and suspicion that was growing within her. She was drained by the end of the day. She knew that sooner or later she would have to confront her husband with her suspicions. If she was right, it would be the end of their marriage. If she was wrong, the mere fact that she could distrust him so would alter the nature of their relationship. Either way that confrontation would initiate some shifting of ground between them, and she was not feeling strong enough yet to take that step.

In the evening they took the boys to see *Pillow Talk* with Doris Day and Rock Hudson at the drive-in. A normal couple on a normal family outing. Sandy meanwhile had been enjoying an afternoon on her own. Ed had a day off and had picked the children up from school to take them for a burger and then bowling. Sandy had cried off saying she was really tired and needed to rest up before her long drive the next day. She had told Ed that she had to make an unscheduled trip to Monterrey to meet with Tony and Chris and it was too much to do the trip in a day, so she would be staying in a motel overnight and be back the next day. She sat in Ed's chair, her feet up on the coffee table, sipping a glass of iced tea.

Sandy had never felt like this with anyone. She had permanent butterflies in the pit of her stomach, and every second thought was a snapshot of Sam – his arms, his flat stomach, his legs. She could shut her eyes and feel the shaft of his penis slipping through her fingers and the velvet smoothness of its tip on her tongue. She sometimes sat trance-like – eyes staring at nothing in front of her. Sometimes a half hour would pass thus with Sandy suspended in this half-world. Never had she been consumed with such longing, never before had she felt so totally suffused with love. She could hear his voice softly in her ear as they made love. The things he said, the way he said them.

Sandy's preparations for her night with Sam were as elaborate and regimented as Esther and Heather's had been for their party. Hair, nails, legs, make-up, what to wear, what to take (she had bought a new nightie, a soft, silky peach colour which was at once revealing and concealing, the kind of nightie that did not stay on for long). These all needed to be timetabled around her family routine, of meals, homework, piano practice, organising the household for the time she would be away. She wouldn't have much time the next morning, between getting the kids ready for their day and sorting out meals and shopping before she and Sam were to set off. She was in the middle of doing her nails when the phone rang. She picked up the receiver gingerly, so as not to smudge the wet polish, and waved the other hand in the air. It was Rose. She had finally confided in Rose a few days before. They had taken Jamie and Heather and Dilly and Esther roller-skating in Polanco Park. This was just a small park with benches and trees with flowers growing around them. The best thing about it was that there was a nice, even pavement all around it, perfect for roller-skating, and Sandy and Rose could keep an eye on the children all the time without having to move from their bench. Rose had brought a thermos of tea and they had bought some elephant's ears pastries at the little bakery nearby. They sat in the shade and chatted. Rose had been so good, so calm and understanding, not at all judgemental as Sandy had feared.

"Listen, Sandy," she had said, "you're my friend and I'm here for you if you need me. All I ask is that you never ask me to lie for you or put me in a position where I have to cover for you. It would just be too awkward, being neighbours and all."

Now on the phone Rose wanted to know if she and Ed wanted to take in a movie with her and Peter that evening. Sandy told her that she was on her own, making her preparations for the next day.

"Do be careful, Sandy, won't you?" she said and the concern in Rose's voice irritated Sandy, who did not want the little bubble she was in to burst with the prick of a reminder that she was playing with fire and had everything to lose.

After she hung up, she turned her attention to her toenails. She placed some cotton wool between the toes and carefully applied the frosted pink nail polish to each delicate nail. The phone rang again. She picked it up and held it between her shoulder and her chin in order to continue painting her nails.

It was Sam.

"Is that the Siren of Avenida de los Picos?"

Sandy grinned.

"It is. And is that my knight of the kitchen table?"

"It is, so long as it hasn't got any crumbs or maple syrup spilled on it. There's nothing I hate more than a crumby, sticky kitchen table."

They both laughed.

"Look, Sandy, honey. I've got some bad news. Nat's cut short her stay and she's back, she came back this afternoon. She's in a funny kind of mood. I don't know what's the matter, but something sure is bugging her."

"Oh no! Really? Well, never mind. It can't be helped, can it?"

Sandy tried to sound light and cheerful even though everything seemed to collapse in on her, and her face showed the strain of disappointment. She did not want to give Sam a hard time over something he couldn't avoid. She did not want to rant and rave or whine like a hard done by teenager. She did not want to sound like a wife. She had to be the perfect lover.

After she hung up, Sandy sat on Ed's chair for a while, deflated, depressed, fighting back the tears that would make her new mascara run and smudge her face, so carefully made up as a dry run for tomorrow. It was four o'clock, three hours before Ed and the kids would return for supper. She phoned Sam back. When she was put through by his secretary, he answered the phone with his business-like voice.

"I'm coming over," she said and hung up.

Sam had been working at some drawings, stencilling in various measurements and instructions. He had a meeting scheduled for 4.30 with one of the partners. He got on the intercom to his secretary asking her to postpone it until the following day. He looked out of his window. It was the rainy season and there was always a shower at this time of day. The geraniums and bougainvillea on his balcony caught the raindrops like diamonds which glistened in the sun and there was a rainbow spanning Chapultepec park. Half an hour later Sandy walked into his office. She was wearing a raincoat and black patent high-heeled shoes. As she walked towards his desk, she unbuttoned and shrugged off the raincoat. The silk of the peach nightie floated around the curves of her body, her nipples standing out against the softness of the material. She trailed the raincoat behind her and let it drop to the floor. Sam leapt up and sprang to the door to lock it. When he turned back to her, she was leaning over his desk reading his desk diary.

"Oh deary me," she said in a sing-song voice, "I see you had to change a little appointment here. I do hope I'm not putting you to any inconvenience, Mr Puchetti."

Her nightie only just covered her behind. Sam leaned against the door, arms folded, admiring her beautiful ankles, her long legs. He came over to the desk and, kneeled down between her legs. He ran his tongue up the inside of her thigh and down the other. He caressed her buttocks and kissed the crease where they met the tops of her thighs. She smelled of perfume and sex. His hands wandered up and down her body, feeling the fullness of her breasts, the mound of her stomach, the silky tangle of her pubic hair. Sandy kept on reading from his diary in her baby doll voice.

"Oohh. I see here that you have to be on site at six o'clock in all that nasty dirt with all those men in their hard hats."

Sam shook off his loafers and undid his trousers which fell to the floor. He slipped off his boxer shorts. His penis, erect, urgent, explored the delicate folds between Sandy's legs. She turned around now, smiling.

"Why, hello there, Mr President."

"Hello," he said, his voice thick with desire. His lips were soft on her neck, on her shoulders, on her breasts. He caressed one of her breasts, licking the nipple gently, with little flicks of his tongue, feeling it grow harder before taking it into his mouth ... His hands travelled down her body, sending little shocks of pleasure through him as he went from her narrow waist to the fullness of the two spheres of her behind which he clutched as his penis continued its gentle exploration. They lowered themselves onto one of the rugs Sandy had bought for him and she wrapped her legs around him. Their lovemaking had an urgency about it and with the added element of danger, that at any moment someone could knock on the door, they came together quickly with an intensity neither could have imagined a few weeks before.

When they looked around the room, they had to laugh at the scene of cast off clothing, the pile of desk paraphernalia scattered about the place, the impeccable orderliness of the rest of the office and the reflection in the balcony door of themselves intertwined on Sam's rug.

As she left, Sandy opened the office door and called behind her: "Thank you, Mr Puchetti. Please give me a call when you have finished those drawings of the kitchen and we'll book another session. Bye now!"

And she chirped a "Good afternoon!" as she passed the receptionist's desk in the foyer.

Lupe, Pedro and Arturo take advantage of a weekend when the family are away in Cuernavaca and travel up to see Margarita and Lupe's brothers. Even though it is only a few hours' drive from the city, it is a journey they cannot make with any frequency, what with the demands of their jobs in the Puchetti household.

Pedro is careful to set the timer on the sprinklers so that his vegetable patch doesn't suffer in the heat and douses the flower beds early in the morning before they set off for the bus station. Margarita has only seen her grandson two or three times a year and his uncles even less, especially Jesús who is now an apprentice surveyor and is often visiting sites when they do visit. Over the years, thanks to Lupe and Pedro's salaries, and of course Gustavo's generous contributions towards Miguel Ángel's schooling amongst other things, the shack has been transformed into a whitewashed abode of three rooms and a separate kitchen. Pedro has erected a picket fence around the house and created a small garden at the front and a vegetable patch at the back for Margarita to tend. Next to this an orange tree shades a small patio peppered with earthenware pots of herbs and pretty flowers. Margarita sits here at a small table mending the cuffs of one of Miguel Ángel's shirts whilst he picks some tomatoes and greens from the vegetable patch and Jesús sets up the table for the banquet they will enjoy later on. The three of them generate a buzz of excitement at the prospect of this family reunion.

Finally, with a whoop and much laughter Lupe and her family arrive and Margarita sweeps Arturo into her arms and showers him with kisses in spite of his protestations. She embraces her daughter and Pedro in turn and then sets to offering a beer, some lemonade, and bowls of nuts. She cannot stop smiling and is transfixed by her grandson, his beauty, his cleverness and how much he resembles her husband. A fleeting stab of sadness that Alfredo cannot witness this scene causes her to pause as she fills a tray with glasses and bowls. She recovers herself before re-emerging onto the patio with refreshments.

"Don't spoil your appetites, we're eating in an hour!"

Lupe is concerned about her mother. She looks worn out and doesn't have the usual bustle in her movements. She breathes unevenly with the slightest exertion and her lips have a bluish tinge to them. In her last letter to Lupe, Margarita had mentioned going to the medical centre. Her usual concoction of herbs and spices didn't seem to be working on her extreme fatigue.

"Mamá, what did the doctors say?"

Margarita makes a dismissive gesture to brush away any talk that would put a pall on the weekend's proceedings, but Lupe presses her.

"I'm worried Mamá. You look tired. What is it?"

Jesús helps himself to some nuts and drains his glass of beer.

"It's her heart. Mamá has a heart condition, and the doctor says she must rest when she is tired."

"Oh, you do overdramatise Jesús!" Margarita shoots a warning glance at him and shakes her head, but he ignores her.

"Yes," he continues, "some days she can't even make it to the market. The doctors have given her some pills, but you will see the medicine is untouched in the kitchen cupboard. Maybe you can convince her to take it!"

Lupe could see her mother's discomfiture at her health condition being so aired in public, especially with Pedro and her sons sitting there. But later that evening whilst they were alone in the kitchen, she pulled out the old captain's chair from the table.

"I'll finish the dishes Mamá, come and sit down."

She motions to her mother to sit. The chair nearly swallows her up. It was as if she had shrunk, and she looks so fragile. Lupe puts the bottle of pills and a glass of water on the table.

"Take it Mamá. You must. The doctors know best, and it will make you feel better."

Margarita, like a sulky child, grudgingly takes the tablet that Lupe offered her.

"There! You must promise me that you will take your medicine Mamá. And when you finish them you must go back to the medical centre and get some more. You can't carry on like this, looking after the house and Miguel Ángel and trudging to the market every day."

Margarita agrees. It was all getting too much for her. But how was she to make ends meet without the proceeds from her tortillas?

"How about asking your friend Luz to help? She goes to the market every day to sell her fruit and vegetables. Why not ask her to sell your tortillas for you? You can give her a share of your profits. Jesús will qualify in a few months and will be earning well and in the meantime Pedro and I can make up any shortfall. You have to slow down, and you must listen to the doctors. Do you understand?"

Margarita sighs and nods her head miserably. She realises that there was a danger Lupe would decide to give up all her opportunities in the city to move back home and take charge. Even though she would love to have her grandson and his parents live there, she would feel so guilty that they would be sacrificing a better life and brighter future for Arturo in the big city.

That night after the rest of the family had retired, Lupe and Pedro sat together on the patio whispering to each other so as not to disturb the rest of the family. Lupe was weeping silently into a bunched-up tissue and Pedro couldn't bear to see her in such distress.

"My mother will die for certain if she doesn't take her medicine and go for her check-ups. She is so stubborn I could scream!"

"I know he's still a kid, but I'm sure Miguel Ángel can take some responsibility to make sure she is taking her medicine, and what about this Luz you were talking about? Could she not help a bit to go along with your mother when she has an appointment at the medical centre?"

"I suppose I could ask her. They have been friends for a long time and Mamá trusts her. I'll go down to her tomorrow and talk to her about it. But this is all short-term stuff! What if she gets worse?"

"Look my love, no one except God knows what the future holds. She could go on forever, as you said, she is so stubborn!"

At this Lupe laughed through her tears and blew her nose.

"And actually, I have been giving a great deal of thought into our own predicament. I don't like the way this affair of el Señor is panning out. From my perspective it is not dying away, and it could end badly for the family and for our jobs."

Lupe looked alarmed.

"Yes. It could come to that, and in any case, I am not happy living and working in this atmosphere of rows and deceit. Perhaps we should be thinking of moving on. We could move up here to be with your mother and between us we have enough experience to get jobs in the town, especially because I am sure we would get glowing references. I could set up a little gardening and landscaping business."

"What about me? There isn't much call for domestic servants around these parts, that's for sure. What could I do?"

"Think of all the things you have to do and you don't even give it a second thought! You are a superb cook, you organise a household, you juggle caring for the family and Arturo and me! You are loyal, trustworthy, efficient, creative and quick to learn, all qualities any employer would appreciate. We have time to plan this. We can buy a typewriter and you can learn to type! You could work in an office or a shop or a restaurant or even a school. Don't be afraid of change, mi amor! It could be the best thing for our little family."

Lupe sat up straight in the captain's chair. Pedro was right. She wasn't that little 16-year-old schoolgirl who had arrived in the big city all those years ago. She was a young woman, a wife, a mother, resourceful and desperate to make the most of her life and that of her son. They returned to the City with a short-term plan.

The following Sunday Lupe, Pedro and Arturo took the bus to La Lagunilla flea market. They held on tight to their money and Arturo's hand and wandered up and down the rows of vendors' stalls, selling everything from wedding dresses to old lawnmowers. They went past one stall which sold a cornucopia of office goods, desk lamps, desk chairs, bundles of stationery, typewriters and accessories. Pedro spotted an Olivetti portable typewriter high up on a shelf, which looked in pretty good condition and was priced at 50 pesos. They carried on walking by till they reached the end of the row then he drew Lupe to him, speaking in a low voice.

"Ok I've seen a good one back there. It's 50 pesos, but I reckon if we play the game, we can get the vendor to drop the price. You go first and see if you can bargain him down to 30. If not, just walk away. We'll go and have an ice cream and come back just before they start packing up. He may be more desperate for a sale by then."

Lupe strolled by on her own. She pointed to the typewriter.

"*Cuánto*?" she asked pretending not to see the price which was helpfully displayed in the platan of the machine. The vendor barely looked at her and merely pointed to the sheet the number was written on.

"I'll give you 25."

"No, maybe 45," the vendor said, perked up a bit, smelling a sale.

"I could go to 30?"

"Sorry, the best I can do is 40."

"Oh well. Thanks anyway," Lupe said and walked away and re-joined Arturo and Pedro by the ice cream vendor at the corner of a nearby square.

They strolled around the market admiring the antiquities and bought Arturo a second-hand leather satchel for school. As the stallholders started showing signs of packing up, Pedro returned to the office stall.

"Hey man, that typewriter there on the shelf, how much?"

The paper now read 45 pesos.

The vendor waved towards the piece of paper.

"I'll give you 25."

"Have a heart, a fellow has to earn his keep. It's a good typewriter! Tell you what, for you I'll come down to 40.

"Make it 30."

"Sorry. No can do, but let's call it 35 and I'll throw in a new ribbon."

The vendor took the typewriter down from the shelf and typed out two or three lines to show that all the parts were functioning.

"Done!" smiled Pedro and they shook hands and Pedro parted with his cash, happy to have made a good deal. He returned, beaming, to Lupe and Arturo and they admired the machine together before putting it in its case and heading for the bus stop.

"Our future starts here!" he cried, hugging his wife and ruffling Arturo's hair as the bus bounced along the road taking them out of the centre and on to Lomas.

The Christmas holidays, a whole two weeks, were a mixed blessing for Esther. Sure, there was the promise of sunny days swimming at the sports club and barbeques and picnic trips out of the city, but without the framework of school she would not see so much of Zac. The times and the place dictated that her parents know her every move, but love made even Esther, normally so well-behaved and sensible, reckless to the point of folly. She would have to learn the gentle art of deception. She knew she would feel guilty deceiving her parents, but what was she to do? She loved Zac and a little guilt was a small price to pay for spending some time together. And so she began to tell half-truths.

"A group of us are going to the movies" was really just her and Zac. She just had to make sure she had a pee before she went so she did not have to use the toilets. The Eccelston Girl neon sign still flickered on and off in her mind. She wove her web of lies carefully, with all the forward planning of a general planning strategies for a battle.

"Lina, Roxy, Maisie and I are going to Chapultepec," she would say, and phone every one of them beforehand to warn them not to phone her whilst she was out and give the game away. The more names she mentioned, the more Rose could relax knowing that there was safety in numbers and anyway, Esther was so sensible, so long as she remained within the parameters of a phone call home at some point during her absence, and a set time to return, Esther knew her secret was safe.

So it was that one day she and Zac went for a stroll in Chapultepec Park. They had a picnic under a tree and watched the balloon sellers pace up and down the walkways. Every now and then the piercing sound of their whistles advertising their presence would silence the cooing of the doves and the chatter of the little sparrows who hopped happily from bench to bench picking at crumbs left on the ground by picnickers. Esther and Zac lay in the grass beneath a tree staring up at the branches, the sun pierced through the heavy foliage and cast a dappled light onto the grass where they lay. They held hands, and every now and then Zac would lean on his elbow and run a blade of grass over Esther, starting in the dark curls which framed her face, down her pale cheeks with their fine peppering of freckles, down her neck and over her bare shoulders. He would then return the blade of grass the same way and brush it gently over her lips until she smiled, and then he would kiss her. Esther lifted her slender arms and wrapped them around his neck. They would kiss, eyes shut, mouths shut, with a tender passion, until their lips were sore. When they sat up again, squinting in the glare of the sun's rays, a couple had taken the bench opposite them, facing the boating lake. On a paved area further on, people sat at tables near a little café. Mothers with their children, elderly couples, tourists, all chatting about their own worlds, their friends, their relations, their homes, their problems. Students talked about their studies or their conquests, and businessmen sat in their suits discussing finance and budgets and gross output. Suddenly Esther sat bolt upright and stared ahead of her.

"What's up?" Zac had sensed the urgency of the movement.

"Oh, uh, nothing. I, I just thought I saw someone I knew, that's all," she stammered.

"We've got to go, Zac," she said. "Mom will have a cow and a half if I'm late."

They got up to go, brushing grass off their clothes. As they passed the park bench, Esther cast a glance at the couple seated there. No. She wasn't seeing things. That was Mr Puchetti, and Heather's Mom, with their arms around each other and his tongue in her mouth, they sure didn't look like just plain ol' neighbours to her.

Esther went straight up to her room when she got home. Rose was busy at the dining room table immersed in bills. She sat with a furrowed brow, pen poised as she ran over a bank statement and entered some figures into a notebook. Esther was relieved to find her mother occupied and therefore unable to question her about her afternoon. She lay on top of her bed. How normal her room seemed. Everything was in its right place, on her side at any rate. How could everything still be so ordinary and in their right place whilst inside she was a churning mass of uncertainty and incomprehension.

She tried to digest the scene she had witnessed in the park. She closed her eyes and pictured them, Heather's mother and Giovanni and Gregorio's father, sitting there kissing on that bench.

112

She did not know what to do with this revelation. She felt a certain complicity in it, after all, she should not have been there either, on her own with Zac. To tell anyone could have disastrous repercussions. Heather's Mom and Dad could get a divorce, Mr Puchetti could leave his wife and the boys. Everything could collapse on Avenida de los Picos and her telling could precipitate the destruction of so many lives. Including hers, because Heather might have to move away, and she would lose her very best friend.

A few years before she had felt a similar guilt at discovering a Christmas present, a doll she had found in a cupboard in her parents' room. She knew it was for her, because she had admired it in the department store during a pre-Christmas shopping trip. She felt bad that she had spoiled the surprise her parents had in store for her, and it cast a cloud over the Christmas preparations. On Christmas morning there was that doll under the tree, but to Esther's delight it said on the card attached to it, and written in elfin writing:

To Esther

From Santa

Esther managed to convince herself that she could not possibly have seen that doll in her parents' room seeing as it was delivered by Santa Claus himself. Her guilt lifted like the morning mist, she felt lighter, carefree again. Now she tried to convince herself that she had not seen Sam and Sandy. In her mind's eye she changed the features of the couple on the bench. She had them sitting apart, she had them looking like two old people. She tried to pretend away the guilty secret she now shared with the two lovers. Esther decided she could not tell anyone at all about this, but she did not know how she would be able to face her best friend, or how to behave normally around Sam and Sandy.

A few weeks later Lupe and Pedro sat in their room during siesta time. It was the day following one of the usual Friday night gatherings. As they had served the party with their drinks and food, passing from kitchen to patio and back again with trays of serving platters glasses and water jugs, they observed the gathering and the interactions between the three couples. They were acutely aware of the tensions which had been sparking between the Señor and the Señora with increasing frequency with arguments and cold silences between them about what appeared to be inconsequential matters. The delay with decorating the extension, Sam forgetting a parents' meeting at the boys' school, Natasha's failure to remember her mother-in-law's dental appointment. They couldn't be in the same room for five minutes without creating a tense atmosphere. Sam was distracted and Natasha looked tired and drawn and she often took her unhappiness out on the boys, shouting at them and sighing in exasperation when they failed to do her bidding.

Now in the privacy of their little room Lupe could vent her spleen.

"Did you see the way he looks at her? And she sits there in a powderpuff cloud of perfume and low necklines with her bosom practically popping out onto the table!"

Lupe cups her own breasts and purses her lips seductively leaning towards her husband. Pedro laughs, delighted at Lupe's playfulness.

"And I also think the Señora Jacob knows something. Her maid told me she overheard her Señora and the blonde one talking in the garden and even though she didn't understand much of what they said, she heard the name of Señor Puchetti on several occasions."

"This is not good for us, cariño." Pedro says, reaching for his wristwatch to check the time. "I don't like the way our life hangs on the fortunes of this family."

Lupe sits on the end of their bed, plaiting her hair and weaving a blue ribbon through it.

"But they have been so good to us over the years. Look how they gave us a home for Arturo and you a job. And what would they do without us? Especially the boys and Señora Puchetti."

"Nothing in life stays the same. The boys are older now and will soon go off like all these gringo kids to some boarding school in America to complete their education. My job as a chauffeur will be less demanding and if the Señores end up divorcing who knows where they would all end up? We need to start planning in earnest so that we have something in place if it all falls apart. And then of course there is your mother."

"Yes," Lupe says and ties a clean apron around her waist and checks herself in the mirror. "Yes, yes, yes, I know! You're right. Well, we should have enough saved to buy you the tools you would need for your gardening and I have reached a good level of proficiency in typing. I need to work on my shorthand, but maybe in four or five months I can bring myself up to speed. Also did I tell you Jesús is now living in the town so if we need to move back home Arturo can share a room with Miguel Ángel and we can sleep in the living room until we can build an extra room for the house. Once we are there it won't take you and Miguel Ángel long to do that and my father's old friend Emilio can help. Anyway, I better get down to the kitchen. Supper won't cook itself, and you ..." she kisses Pedro on his forehead, "you also need to get down to the garden. I need a couple of chilies and tomatoes for my *huevos rancheros*."

Esther's dilemma is resolved a couple of months later. The Jacob family were having supper. Unusually they were all sitting around the dining room table. Supper was normally a light meal, sandwiches or rolls with cheese or a scrambled egg or a salad. The three sisters would sit in the dining room and were allowed to read whilst they ate their supper. Gail usually had her nose immersed in *The Seven Pillars of Wisdom* or some novel by Jane Austen or one of the Brontës, whilst Esther and Dilly read *Archie* comics. Rose and Peter would normally have their supper in the living room, listening to the radio, usually the news or a quiz show was on at this time. Tonight, though, Lupe was making quesadillas. The smell of the tortillas frying wafted from the kitchen and on the table was a bowl each of guacamole, sour cream and *frijoles refritos* which all together created the most delicious taste in the world.

"We're going back to New York."

It was as if a boulder had fallen into the middle of the dining table. Esther had a snapshot image of the family as she looked at each of them in turn. Dilly clapped her hands.

"Tootsie rolls and Three Musketeers!" she cheered at the prospect of her favourite candy bars.

Gail, daintily holding a quesadilla between thumb and forefinger, let it drop back onto her plate. "What about my exams? They might be doing a different syllabus in New York!"

"What about Zac!" cried Esther. "... And Roxy and Maisie and Heather," she reeled off the names of several friends to detract from her original emphasis on Zac.

Dilly, now realising that this was more serious than she first thought started to cry.

"What about Arturo and Cha Cha?" she wailed. Esther put her arms around her whilst the three girls looked accusingly at their father.

"I hate your stupid job, Daddy, it's ruined everything!" Esther said, distraught. "It took us ages to get used to Mexico, and now we have our lovely house and our lovely school and our ..."

Peter shrugged and held out his hands as if to see if it was raining.

"I'm sorry," he said, "it's beyond my control."

He hated upsetting them all.

"I know this is a bit of a shock," Rose intervened, "but we always knew this was a temporary posting. It's just come a bit sooner than expected. But we can come back if we want to, during the summer vacation. The main thing is that we are all together. Look on the bright side. You'll see all of your old New York friends again and we'll be back in our own house!"

A part of Esther, even at that dreadful moment, felt that this was a blessed escape from her present dilemma. Was it better for her to feel wretched because of leaving Zac and school and her friends and her lovely Avenida de los Picos and her precious Mexico, or to feel this ghastly burden of responsibility about Heather's Mom and Sam? By the time they returned for a holiday everything will have blown over and she would not have to keep this horrid secret anymore. Heather was already wondering why Esther was declining invitations to play at her house, even with the lure of brownies and American chocolate. More often than not she would go over to Esther's to do homework and play. Esther gave the excuse that her mother wanted to oversee her schoolwork as her last report card hadn't exactly set the world on fire.

The months passed and then May was a flurry of packing and *despedidas,* farewell parties, for the Jacob family. Mrs Puchetti invited all the children for a farewell picnic in her garden. She wanted to give Esther especially a good send off. Pedro drove her to the big covered market in town where she bought little individual picnic baskets for each of the children, and she instructed Lupe as to what treats to pack into each one. She knew the girls especially would love this little touch, even if the boys were probably too grown up to appreciate her efforts. Each basket held egg salad and ham and cheese sandwiches, grapes and cherries, a bottle of pop, cookies and a chocolate bar. Ice cream would, of course, also be on the menu. Each child also received a little wrapped gift in their basket. Esther was delighted to unwrap another silver charm for her bracelet, a little cocker spaniel to remind her of Cha Cha and Mrs Puchetti. She stayed chatting to the old lady once the picnic had been consumed and the other children had run off to play.

"So, Esther, how do you feel about leaving me and Cha Cha and restarting your life in New York? You must be so looking forward to seeing all your old friends again, no?"

Esther looking down miserably and toying with the new addition to her charm bracelet shook her head.

"No! I hate New York! I love it here! I love my school and my friends and our house and the mountains and and ..." she trailed off as her eyes brimmed with tears.

"Now, now my dear," murmured Mrs Puchetti, handing Esther a napkin to dry her eyes. "As you know, I too have had so many changes in my life. First leaving my village and family in Italy, then leaving Boston to move here. And although I was sad to leave behind my family, my country and all my friends, each move was the start of a new and exciting chapter in my life. Change is always a double-edged sword with both fear of the unknown and excitement for new possibilities. And it will be the same for you little Esther. In a few months you will be right at home as an American teenager!"

At this Esther perked up. Perhaps there were some attractions to moving back, the music scene, the boutiques full of cool clothes, the food, her old friends.

"But I hope you will think of me sometimes and maybe send me a postcard letting me know how you are getting on?"

Esther nodded.

"Yes, course I will. I have some nice stationery so I can send you letters."

"That will be lovely, and I promise to write back with all our news too. Now, véte! Go play with the others!"

The plan was that the Jacobs were going to drive back to New York through Texas and the South then up the east coast and on to New York. On the morning of their departure all the children on Avenida de los Picos lined up next to the '58 Chevy. Zac had come over to say goodbye. He handed a small box to Esther. It contained a pretty silver bracelet with two amethyst

118

stones at the clasp. She gave him a forty-five, "Blue Velvet ", their song. They hugged each other and then he kissed her, right there in front of her parents! The family got into the car and Peter turned on the ignition.

"*Adiós! Hasta la vista, adiós!*"

Their friends ran up the block trying to keep up with the car, calling and waving. The three sisters waved out of the back window as the car picked up speed and they waved until they rounded the corner, and all their friends were gone.

Esther cried all the way to the border, all the way through the desert and into Texas. When they checked into a hotel, her face drained of colour and her eyes puffy and red, she ate cherry pie à la mode with real American chocolate ice cream, and when they switched on the TV, *American Bandstand* featured Lesley Gore – in person! – singing "It's my Party". Maybe being back in the USA wasn't so bad after all. The next day they drove on to New Orleans where they listened to lovely jazzy music and played Marco Polo in the swimming pool of the motel. When they hit Tennessee they saw hundreds of billboards advertising Ruby Falls. "Ruby Falls One Hundred Miles", then "Ruby Falls Fifty Miles" ... "Don't forget to see Ruby Falls 25 Miles" ... "You are about to enter Chattanooga, home of Ruby Falls" – and then, once they left Chattanooga, "Did you see Ruby Falls?". The family would laugh about this memory of their road trip for years afterwards. By the time they reached New York, Esther's heartbreak was now a bearable heartache. She wondered if Douglas had a girlfriend.

The absence of the Jacobs on Avenida de los Picos was keenly felt by Heather, Jamie and the Puchetti boys. Elena stayed on to ready the house for the new tenants and would have continued her employment seamlessly with the new tenants, Mr and Mrs Gantry, as arranged with the landlord. What she hadn't been prepared for was the flock of birds that took up residence with the Gantrys. They frightened the daylights out of her, flying out from unexpected places and brushing her head with their wings as they swooped from curtain pole to chandelier and even settling on her shoulder whilst she dusted and swept. She decided to go back to her village and spend some time with her family before seeking work again. The Gantrys did not concern themselves much with the comings and goings of the neighbours, other than to complain if Heather and Jamie played their music too loud.

"It frightens our birds, dear," Mrs Gantry explained to Sandy, "They get all a-flutter and won't eat."

The Gantrys had no children, just birds – parakeets, love birds, canaries, twenty or thirty of them. The spare room, used for storage by the Jacobs as it was too small for a bedroom, was turned into an aviary, with cages ranged along the walls. Every afternoon at two o'clock, Mrs Gantry would close up all the windows upstairs, and Mr Gantry would do likewise downstairs. When he sounded the all clear, Mrs Gantry would let the birds out of their cages, a swirl of yellows and blues and greys and greens and pinks would fly out of the "aviary" and then dart about in different directions. All the birds had a favourite place in the house. The canaries showed a preference for the living room with its high ceiling. They would swoop and dive and then perch on the curtain rail, chirping appreciatively. The parakeets preferred the sunny breakfast room where they could play hide and seek in the net curtains and peck at any crumbs left on the floor or the table. The love birds liked the coolness of the tiled bathroom. They would take it in turns to stand under the dripping tap in the tub, ruffling their feathers and preening themselves before hopping onto the shelf to admire themselves in the mirror.

Then at 2.30, having cleaned the cages and put fresh newspaper down in them, Mrs Gantry would stand at the top of the stairs and shake the packet of birdseed.

"Come along my lovies, come along my dears. Lunchtime!"

Mr Gantry would go through the rooms with a rolled-up newspaper, coaxing the more reluctant birds down from their perches, and back up to the aviary. Once back in their now pristine cages, they would swing happily on their swings or peck at their little bells and mirrors. In the evenings the Gantrys would let two or three of the birds out to keep them company in the living room They would teach them tricks, like pulling a little cart with a fellow feathery friend in it, or climbing a little ladder onto the coffee table. One of the canaries could talk and Mrs Gantry taught it the first line of "Waltzing Matilda" which it would sing with perfect pitch and then screech "Well blow me down!" – which it must have learnt from a previous owner.

Mrs Puchetti had visited the couple when they moved in to take over a welcoming home-made cake. She soon realised that she was an unwelcome intruder in the Gantrys' daily routine. Mr Gantry had retired from running his own security business, mostly working nights, and he had never got back into the normal rhythms of the day. Consequently, the house was shrouded in darkness with the heavy drapes in the living room and the curtains in the upstairs rooms remaining shut until gone one o'clock when he would rise. It gave visitors the feeling that they were walking into Miss Haversham's house in *Great Expectations*. The furniture was permanently covered in plastic (Mrs Puchetti decided this must be to protect it from the birds) and the piano always had music propped up on its stand, but the keys were yellow with age and no one ever heard a note played on it the whole time they lived there. In her heyday Mrs Gantry had been a show girl in a chorus line, and in spite of her age, her appearance still reflected her former glory. She wore tight, leopard skin pedal pushers and gold or silver lamé tops with matching dangly earrings. Her hair, dyed blonde, was done up with combs into a twist. Her wrists and her freckled hands were weighed down with bangles and rings and her nails were always manicured and painted dark red. She wore lots of make-up, including lipstick to match her nails and false eyelashes, and she wore several gold chains, one of which was attached to her reading glasses which hung over her bosom, above her midriff. Heather was totally fascinated by this apparition, especially her shoes. She would write to Esther about these new, odd neighbours and always comment on Mrs Gantry's shoes. They were the highest stiletto sandals, in gold or silver, depending on which top she was wearing. You could hear her trip-trip tripping all over the tiles and the wooden floors in the house as she went about her daily chores. Mrs Puchetti was fascinated by, but did not totally approve of this woman, who was after all one of her peers, and felt there was something shady about her owl of a husband. She missed the Jacobs, her tea times with Rose, the fun on Friday nights with all the families together. Those times had fallen by the wayside since the Jacobs had gone. Somehow it was not the same without them. Natasha, anyway, had never been the impetus behind them, and Sam did not seem to have any time to socialise these days. She worried about how hard he was working.

Sandy also missed Rose. She had no-one to confide in now, and it wasn't the same in letters. Besides, letters could fall into the wrong hands, with disastrous consequences. She was bursting to tell Rose about the trip she and Sam had planned in November. Four whole nights in Acapulco! The thought of it sustained her through the following weeks and months when it was more tricky for her and Sam to meet because of their work schedules or their family commitments.

Natasha had barely noticed the Jacobs' absence. She liked Rose and had enjoyed their time together visiting exhibits and attending lectures, but she had never really been that close to her – or to anyone else for that matter – she would muse during those spells of time when she would catch herself doing absolutely nothing but staring blankly into space. She would pull herself up sharply and quickly engage in some activity, some task, anything to prevent her dark thoughts from taking possession of her and sending her off again into a kind of frenzy of searching for clues into Sam's imagined "other life".

Over the weeks and months since her abortive trip to Acapulco, she had even begun to doubt her own sanity. She had fabricated a whole fantasy life which she was certain her husband was conducting once he closed the front gates and went to work, or to the club for a game of tennis, or to play cards with his pals. Every time he came home, she would quiz him about his every move. His responses were always plausible, and she would feel at once relieved and then filled with such self-loathing.

"Don't you have anything better to do with your time, your mind, than fabricate an exciting existence for Sam?" she would remonstrate with herself.

She had once been so confident, so sure of herself and his love and admiration for her, and she hated feeling so worthless and needy. She decided it was time to take herself in hand. She needed to show Sam how independent and secure in herself she could be in order to re-gain his respect and admiration. She started to attend more classes at the institute. She signed up for a psychology class, but she soon lost patience with it as it seemed to attract every unhappily married woman in the English-speaking colony of Mexico City. She attended a writers' workshop and had a short story published in *The News*. She heard from a friend in Boston about these "women's groups" which were starting up all over the USA as part of the blossoming women's movement. She was intrigued. What did these women all talk about? All she could think about was Sam's fantasy affair which was all consuming to the exclusion of practically everything else in her life. She saw an advert on the Institute's notice board for women who were interested in starting up such a group to contact a number. She wrote the number down on the back of her hand and phoned when she got home.

Natasha arrived at the first meeting filled with dread and anxiety. A woman of about forty with long brown hair, beautiful grey eyes and a welcoming smile answered the door.

"Hi, you must be Natasha. Come right on in, straight ahead and follow the noise!"

Natasha crossed a patio with terracotta pots of geraniums dotted about on the flagstones. The sound of women talking and occasional laughter wafted out of a room which gave onto the patio through open French doors. Natasha entered a large sunny room comfortably furnished with sofas, armchairs and two leather Moroccan hassocks. The furniture was ranged around a beautiful Mexican rug on a highly polished, dark wooden floor and there was a magnificent fireplace and mantle upon which sat several family photos in ornate silver frames.

"Please sit down," her hostess indicated a space on one of the sofas. "Let me introduce you to everyone."

She pointed to each woman who smiled or nodded in turn and finally pointing to herself with a laugh she said, "and I'm Madi."

The women were about the same age as Natasha, and they seemed to be as nervous as she was which was somehow comforting.

Madi said, "I suppose the first thing we need to decide is what kind of group this should be, you know, what we each hope to get out of our meetings. And then based on that we need to perhaps think about what ground rules, if any, there should be."

Natasha took in the décor of the room, the beautiful floor and flagstone hearth, the wood and leather of the furniture and the thick bottle-green glass top of the coffee table around which they all sat. She studied the faces of each woman as they took it in turn to introduce themselves and spend five uninterrupted minutes talking about themselves and finishing with their reasons for joining the group. Natasha could not remember ever talking about herself for such an extended period of time. She was surprised at how much she was able to say about herself in this room full of strangers.

"I don't really know what I want from the group," she started, staring fixedly at the papier mâché fruit arranged in the clay bowl on the coffee table. "I suppose a safe place to discover whether the worst fears about myself are actually true!"

The others laughed. She had struck a chord of some kind. She began to relax, feeling accepted by her new friends.

They decided on just a few ground rules. No alcohol, no smoking, no interrupting. They would start by devoting an entire session to each woman in turn and, depending on the issues raised in those sessions, devote the following meetings to different topics.

Over the next three weeks Natasha listened to three of the women talking about their lives. One of them was the victim of an abusive husband who thought she was attending a cookery course on these evenings. Another, Geraldine, spent the entire hour talking about her daughter who had committed suicide five years before. The years had not diminished her anguish and the session was filled with long silences and tears, both her own and those of the other women, as she shared her grief with them. Natasha felt at the end of this session, that no matter how different they all were, no matter what different worlds they came from, something special was happening in Madi's living room that bound them all together.

Natasha was relieved that it was not her turn the following week. Her problems, (her imagined problems?) seemed totally frivolous and self-indulgent by comparison. The following week was Jude's turn. She was in her fifties, a striking woman, her pewter hair was held back with two tortoise shell combs and she wore a grey and silver kaftan and an unusual silver necklace with matching earrings. She started by voicing what Natasha had been thinking.

"After last week I honestly did not feel I could come here and twitter on about my life, and I have to admit I almost didn't come tonight."

Geraldine cleared her throat.

"Listen everyone. I just want to say how much the last session helped me. I really feel it was a turning point in my grieving. I know it must have been upsetting for everyone, I know you weren't expecting it. But each of us carries something or things that cause us distress. No one's life and no-one's feelings are trivial. We are all precious, we are all entitled to a voice."

Jude talked about fear. She felt trapped in a perpetual state of paralyzing fear and anxiety about her parents, her children, her future with a husband who, after twenty-six years of marriage, had decided that he was homosexual and wanted the freedom to explore this revelation.

"I mean it calls into question everything I have taken as solid, as real, for my entire adult life. Who is this guy I married? Was anything he ever said to me true? Was he thinking of other men when he made love to me? How could I not have known?"

The following week it was Natasha's turn. She started her session with a description of her New England upbringing and her family. She was surprised at the memories which welled up and spilled out of her mouth — a party which she missed because of the mumps, carefree

125

holidays in the Hamptons, her Dad's Victorian values, her mother's sweet nature and how she always acted as a buffer between her and her volatile father, and her father's refusal to attend her wedding because he disapproved of Sam and his nebulous Italian provenance. She talked about her children and she talked about Sam and she talked and talked. And when she had finished talking, she felt a tremendous relief that she was at last able to share her misery and voice her fears about Sam.

"So how long do you want to go on feeling like this?" Madi continued, "I think that women have a gut sense when something is not right and most of the time they are sadly proved right."

The other women nodded in agreement.

Laura helped herself to one of the biscuits from a plate on the coffee table.

"You know, I once had a boyfriend who lied to me for months about his cheating, even though I knew, I just knew something was up. It made me feel a bit crazy that I was imagining things, and we just started having endless arguments."

"And, so, what did you do about it?" Natasha turned to Laura, hoping for advice as to what she should do.

"I walked! I had just had enough and realised that anything would be better than feeling like that. So worthless, so suspicious, so angry all the time. I finally had the courage to break it off and then heard from several so-called friends that they had known all along but didn't feel it was their place to tell me! And although I was broken hearted, it was better than feeling the way I had, a big relief. The worse thing for me wasn't just his cheating, it was knowing that everyone else knew and that made me feel so stupid and ashamed.

Natasha decided that she had to confront Sam once and for all. He was going on a business trip to Guatemala for a few days. At least if he was out of the country with one of the partners, he couldn't be with anyone else. Natasha could relax for a few days. She would confront him when he returned.

The Jacobs settled back into their New York home and their New York routine. To all intents and purposes, nothing much had changed but all of Esther's friends were now heavily into adolescence. Whereas Esther thought that she was really moving in the fast lane by telling the occasional fib to her parents in order to see Zac, her friends back in New York had gone into orbit. Going on a trip did not mean going to Jones Beach, "going out with" meant making out with. Esther's girlfriends fell into two categories, the in crowd or the dorks. She felt safer as a dork and consequently spent evenings and weekends at home studying or writing to Zac or Heather about her misery.

147-444 Village Road

Queens

1st October 1965

Dear Heather,

Hello old bean. What ho! How is everything with you and MARK (or is it Raúl now, you naughty girl!). Nothing is new here. I hate New York. Everything's changed. All my friends are freaks and New York is sooooo scary! I'm afraid to go anywhere on my own. I actually take the school bus cos I'm too scared of the subway, and all the boys here are on drugs and all the girls are fast. I don't do anything! I come home from school, I do my homework, I have supper, I watch Bonanza (in English!) or Leave it to Beaver and then I go to bed. That's my life! We live all the way out here in the sticks and everything's happening in Manhattan and I'm so chicken I don't even want to stay with my friends in town in case I get knifed or raped in their apartment. I wish I could be in my beautiful Mexico. I miss everyone, especially you and Zac. He wrote and said he loved me – isn't that just boss! Isn't he just dreamy? And he's such a nice guy, not like the boys here. I hate them. Dilly has grown about two feet since we got back here. Mom reckons the altitude must have stunted her growth. Gail is going to go to college in London. Can you imagine? I'll have a sister living right near Carnaby Street! Maybe she'll even see George who, as you know, is the BEST BEATLE OF THEM ALL!!! She's sooo lucky. Oh, Heather! Everything is changing, everything except me, that is. How's your pesky little brother and the dog? Say hi to your Mom and Dad and to my beautiful house. Play your record player real loud so the birds can have a good old dance around! Can't wait to see you again whenever that is!

Love,

Esther

P.S. Don't you think Patti Boyd is really not George's type? I see him with a brunette, myself.

223 Avenida de los Picos

Lomas

Mexico

20th October 1965

Dear Est,

Toodle pip chaps! Gotcha letter yesterday. Believe me things aren't much better here. Life is not the same without you, ma chère amie. And Mark is history. I caught him kissing Marsha at a party last week. I totally flipped! So, I'm back with Jorge again. He's so sharp. Romances around town:

Roxy and Invar. He's taking her to the American School party.

David and Andrea dance together all the time, but Mike is coming back from the US at Christmas, so I don't know what he will have to say! I LOVE "Baby's in Black". Have you heard

George's twangy guitar in it? They are playing it every two minutes on Radio Ciudad. Mom and Dad are still fighting over stupid things, but they did go out for a romantic meal for their anniversary the other night, so I'm not too worried. Those people in your house are just weirder than the Twilight Zone, you know? You know the movie The Birds? It's a bit like that next door. So boring and they don't have any kids. Jamie and I still go over to the Puchettis' sometimes to play with Gregorio and Giovanni and Arturo, but it's not the same without you guys. Anyway, I must buzz off. Mom's having a cow and is nagging me to do my French ... Thornbull, of course, more verbs!

Au revoir ma petite amie,

Heather

P.S. Okay. George does have a nice smile, but Paul is cuter.

12 Casa de Rosas

Lomas, Mexico

28th October 1965

Querida Est,

I miss you. Nothing here is the same since you left. Roxy had a party on Saturday and some kids from the American School gate crashed-they had beer and tequila, and everyone got totally smashed. Mark got off with Marsha and Heather spent yet another party bawling in the bathroom. I danced with Mimi, but it wasn't the same as with you. My parents are talking about sending me and my brother to boarding school in Florida! I shall fight it to the death though, after what you say about the good old USA. But at least we would be on the same side of the continent. I still love you. Does your hair still frizz in the rain?

Zac

147-44 Village Road

Queens

11th November 1965

Dear Zac,

Glad to hear you may be nearer, even if it is Florida. We drove through Florida on our road trip here and it's really cool (or rather hot!!) and the ocean there is so warm … like taking a bath! Maybe you can visit New York some time. I miss you so much and play our song all the time I don't go to any parties or dances 'cos all my friends live in Manhattan and there is no way I can ask my Dad to drive all the way into town to come pick me up. So, I live the life of a nun … boring! Nothing exciting happens around here. I just do my homework and listen to my transistor radio , especially Cousin Brucie's show! I have to do an English composition on "something that changed your life" by tomorrow so will write again at the weekend. Maybe I'll write my composition about you!

Love,

Esther

She wrote this letter on her special stationery and carefully slipped it, together with a lock of her hair, into the envelope. She addressed it and then turned it over and wrote SWALK on the other side. She then put on some of her mother's lipstick and left a big red kiss on the envelope.

226 Avenida de los Picos

Lomas

Mexico

13th November 1965

My dear little Esther,

I hope this letter finds you and your family well and all settled back in your home in New York. I imagine it all takes a bit of getting used to, not least because of the weather. I see a blizzard is expected over there, but here, as always, the skies are blue and the sun shines brilliantly. I just need a little cardigan over my shoulders if we sit out in the evenings.

We all miss you and the family very much. Avenida de los Picos seems so much quieter without you and your sisters though goodness knows Gregorio and Giovanni manage to fill the air with their arguing and shouting from morning to night! I miss your mother's visits and also our little chats, and I try to imagine your life in the big city. I am sure next time we meet you will have grown taller and turned into quite the young girl about town! Lupe and Pedro have asked me to send their regards and Arturo sends the enclosed photograph of himself with Cha Cha for Dilly so she doesn't forget them.

Do write me a nice newsy letter back dear Esther and give my very best to your parents, won't you?

Abrazos,

Eva Puchetti

"Hello Sandy? Can you talk?"

Sam was in his office.

"Yes. Did you get the tickets?"

"I'm looking at them now! Two tickets for Acapulco, and I managed the honeymoon suite at the Paradiso."

"How wonderful," Sandy said, sitting on the sofa hugging a cushion to her whilst admiring her newly painted toenails – "Vamp Red" – which contrasted with the milky whiteness of her delicate feet.

"What time do we leave?"

"We take off at five tomorrow, returning about lunchtime on Friday."

"Four whole nights!" she sighed. "Four whole nights all to ourselves. I sure hope nothing goes wrong this time."

"You packed yet?"

"No. I'll do it tomorrow once Ed and the kids have left. Ed may wonder why I'm packing little silky things for a business trip to the border!"

Sam smiled at the thought of those silky things on Sandy's beautiful body.

"Oh, oh," he whispered, "you're getting me going here!"

Sandy cooed: "Oh Mr President, you'll just have to be patient, won't you?"

"I'll take a cab to Polanco. You pick me up at the corner nearest the market, okay?"

"Can't wait. See you tomorrow. I love you!"

"Love you too!" Sam hung up. His smile disappeared as he sat upright in his chair and dialled home.

"Nat? It's me. I'll be home in about an hour. I have a few last-minute details to attend to here. You and the kids go ahead with supper without me. I'll get there as soon as I can."

It was such a strain talking to his wife these days. She was more distant than ever and more involved with her own things – classes, women's groups – there was hardly any space left for him. No wonder he had to turn to someone else. He tried to remember what it was that had attracted him to Natasha in the first place. He supposed it was that she was so different to him. It was funny how the very thing that had first attracted him was now partly the cause of the breakdown of his relationship with her. He hated deceiving her, but he hated her for making him deceive her. He tidied his desk and rolled up his drawings. He locked his office door. When he arrived home, supper was over, the boys were playing basketball with Arturo and Natasha had gone to a meeting. Lupe made him some soup and a sandwich. He packed his bag and hid the airline tickets in an envelope under the lining at the bottom of his briefcase. He stuffed his bathing trunks into a shoe. He would slip his shorts and sandals in at the last minute. Natasha might wonder why he was packing beachwear for a business trip.

It was one of those bitterly cold weekends. The normal New York sounds were muffled by the recent fall of snow which covered all the roads in a fine powder. Esther could hear the jingling of the snow chains on the cars as they rumbled down her street, slowly, slowly, so as not to skid.

A fire engine siren sounded down on Union Turnpike. The falling snow distorted the sound which rose and was lost in the dense white cloud which hung over the city. Esther watched from her bedroom window as some younger children built a fort in preparation for an afternoon's game of "War". The village was built around a series of courts around which the two storey apartment blocks were built. The kids from the next court over on the other side of the playground were busy making their own preparations. Their calls and laughter bounced off the sides of the houses and snow-laden trees. The snow began to fall again. Thick, luscious flakes which tapped against the windowpane.

Esther sat at her desk. She wore what she called her "study" outfit, an extraordinary combination of garments – woolly knee socks, a sleeveless summer dress under which she wore a turtleneck jumper and to top it all, an orange and green woolly hat within which the frizz of her hair was confined. She bent over her French homework for Mrs Longman. It had been due in the week before, but something extraordinary had happened and she had the most unique excuse for not handing it in. Esther had left school late that day. There were rehearsals for the school play, *The Crucible*. She was playing the part of Betty.

"Basically, I spend the first three scenes in a catatonic state in bed and then I freak out in scene four," she wrote to Mrs Puchetti in her reply to her last letter. She was forced to take the public bus home from the 59th Street bridge into Queens. It was like a slow boat to China, but nothing would induce her to take the subway. It was dark at 5.15 and the bus was halfway over the bridge when suddenly the world was plunged into darkness. The only lights came from car headlights. Manhattan was shrouded in darkness. The UN Building on the river stood out against the skyline, behind it the outline of the Empire State and the Chrysler buildings looked like witches' fingers jabbing into the night sky. A ribbon of silver snaked its way up FDR Drive. Ahead of her, on the other side of the river, the Silvercup sign on the bread factory had gone out and beyond that an uncanny and eerie darkness veiled the Borough of Queens. The bus passengers looked at each other for confirmation that there was in fact a blackout of New York City. It took a few minutes for people to lose their usual New York "don't give anything away" travel faces, however the bus driver called over his shoulder. "Holy Moses! Where's all the lights?" and suddenly everyone was talking.

The traffic began to slow to a snail's pace and the bus came to a stop under the EL. The sound of police and fire sirens and car horns filled the air. Esther looked out the window at her favourite store – a bridal shop – it always had a beautiful fairy-tale display in the window of a happy bride in a gorgeous white and frilly creation. The bride stood out now, shimmering, like a phantom in the gathering gloom. Esther saw some amazing sights on her way home. Ordinary people doing extraordinary things like directing the traffic or drivers picking complete strangers up from bus stops and outside the subway stations. They passed the huge cemetery on Queens Boulevard. It filled Esther with dread, and she had a superstition that in order to dispel the hex this place might put on her or her family, she had to hold her breath from one end of the cemetery to the other, and she prayed there wouldn't be a red light in the middle to hold the bus up forcing her to take a breath. Tonight, she knew this would not be possible, so she shut her eyes instead, opening just once to check that the bus had cleared that particular obstacle. The massive statue of Christ on the cross loomed over her in the dark. She wished she was home, chatting to her mother about her day over a cup of hot chocolate and a cupcake. The bus crawled on to Forest Hills, across Main Street and down Union Turnpike. It was 7.00 pm by the time she got home. Her mother and sisters were sitting in the living room which was lit by two candles. The transistor radio was on giving regular bulletins about the blackout and they listened as they ate a supper of chicken noodle soup and saltine crackers. Rose was worried about Peter getting down the 35 floors of the building in which he worked. At around eleven o'clock he finally opened the front door with his usual cheery "I'm home!".

Rose gasped with relief and once he had removed his coat and hat, she held him and he kissed her.

"I'm fine," he murmured, "It's ok."

The sisters were relieved. They were all safe now and could enjoy the excitement of the emergency.

"What about my French homework?" Esther suddenly cried.

"I'm sure your teacher will understand Est," soothed Rose, "after all it's not every day that New York has a blackout!"

Esther sighed now as she tackled the French homework. Her radio was as usual tuned to WABC with Cousin Brucie playing all the latest and the grooviest hits. She turned it up when the Beatles began to sing "If I Fell" and hummed along to it as she leafed through her French-English dictionary.

Rose hovered outside Esther's bedroom door. Clutching a letter in her hand she hesitated as she watched the back of her daughter's head as she bent over her homework. There was something at once comical and vulnerable about this apparition in the woolly hat. Rose bit her bottom lip, took a deep breath and entered the room.

"Est honey?"

Esther turned around. Her mother's voice immediately alerted her to some unknown dread.

"Sweetie, can you turn off the radio for a minute and come sit here with me?"

Loss

Sandy picked Sam up in a cab on the corner of the park. In spite of a torrent of rain they arrived in good time at the airport and had a glass of wine in the bar before boarding the five o'clock flight to Acapulco.

Sam squeezed her hand as the plane took off and reached altitude. Meanwhile Natasha had spent the afternoon clearing out cupboards and chests of drawers. The extension was finally finished and ready for the boys to occupy and it was a good excuse to get rid of old clothes, broken toys endless sports equipment, books and old school bags and comics. She had it all organised into separate piles for throwing out, giving away or for the school jumble sale. She sat now in an old pair of dungarees and tee shirt, her curls escaping wildly from the headscarf she had donned for the dusty, dirty job. She was sitting opposite her mother-in-law, sipping from a glass of cold lemonade, enjoying the cool of the late afternoon and the view of the garden where Arturo was playing a game of chase the ball with Cha Cha. The two women chuckled occasionally at the antics of boy and dog as they ran around the trees and shrubbery.

"My room could do with a tidy you know," observed Mrs Puchetti, hoping to catch her daughter-in-law in a magnanimous mood.

"I have stuff even from Italy in my cupboards. And the suitcases on top of the wardrobes are full of old photographs and diaries and letters from my parents."

At this Natasha perked up.

"Really? Diaries? Gosh they would be so interesting to read!"

Natasha knew the story of her mother-in-law's life in Italy and her escape from grief and poverty to the USA, but diaries and photographs and letters? They could make for interesting fodder for a short story or even a book!

"Would you be willing to look at them with me?"

Mrs Puchetti was at an age where getting rid of the accumulation of 80 odd years' worth of "stuff" was as pleasurable to her as accumulating "stuff" was to the younger generations like

Natasha ... especially Natasha! She fretted about reaching a stage where she had no control over what should be kept and what could be dispatched to the maid and her family or the ragman or the garbage. Also, there were some items of jewellery and silverware and she wanted to make sure Natasha and Sam knew the stories behind them and how valuable they were before she herself couldn't remember.

She smiled like a crocodile basking in the sun.

"I would be delighted to show them to you!"

They both sipped their lemonades contentedly. It was a rare moment of peace and affection between the two women. The phone rang behind them and Natasha reluctantly got up from her seat and disappeared into the cool darkness of the living room. Mrs Puchetti helped herself to an almond biscuit and was at first oblivious to the conversation going on behind her. Then she heard Natasha saying.

"I'm afraid you have made a mistake. My husband is in Guatemala, he wasn't flying to Acapulco."

Mrs Puchetti straightened up in her chair alerted to the tone of Natasha's voice.

"No, I'm sorry, there must be some mistake," Natasha hung up and re-emerged onto the patio,

"That's strange. The airline is calling about a ticket issued for Acapulco that has Sam's details on it. They said they were phoning the contact number given which was his office for some reason, and his secretary gave them his home number."

"But he is going to Guatemala, no? That's what he told me too."

Natasha went back to the phone and lifting the receiver, rang Sam's office. All Mrs Puchetti could hear was the rise and fall of Natasha's voice as she spoke to his secretary. A few minutes later she emerged and sat heavily opposite her mother-in-law. She was so pale, and her hands trembled as she reached for Mrs Puchetti's hand.

"His secretary said that she only knew that Sam was taking a few days off and she didn't know anything about a project in Guatemala."

Mrs Puchetti held tight to Natasha's hand as a bolt of sheer dread suffused her whole being, freezing the very marrow of her bones. She couldn't make out what Natasha was saying to her as the shrill humming of the cicadas filled her ears. It was as if she and her daughter-in-law were trying to communicate under water, every time they bobbed up for air, she would hear the odd word and then submerge her head again

"Ticket … plane … airport … field … Sam … Sam … Sam …"

Mrs Puchetti took a big gasp of air.

"My Sam??? My son?"

Alerted by this anguished cry, Lupe and Pedro rushed from the kitchen where they had been preparing the evening meal. They tried to make sense of the scene of the two distraught women and the odd words they were able to catch in between sobs.

Lupe went from one to the other putting her arms around first Natasha and then the old woman, wiping her own tears with her apron and murmuring comforting words whilst Pedro hung back not knowing quite what to do but already thinking about the practicalities of how they would tell the boys about el Señor. They were due to return from basketball practice within the hour and Arturo, attracted by the commotion, had begun wandering over to the patio where this scene was playing out.

Over the next few hours there was pandemonium. Gregorio and Giovanni arrived home and were thrown headlong into the maelstrom of grief. The boys and Mrs Puchetti were inconsolable whilst Natasha sat in a chair like a statue, sometimes staring in front of her, sometimes with a puzzled expression on her face and muttering to herself. Pedro took Arturo to the kitchen where he tried to explain what he gathered had happened to Señor Puchetti. Meanwhile Lupe darted in and out of the kitchen taking food and drinks out to the family who were still sitting on the patio and standing by, distraught herself, in case they needed anything. Her heart broke for the two boys, her own father's shocking demise still so fresh in her memory. She knew what they were going through and how that grief would play out over the days and weeks to come. The next few hours were a blur. Natasha and Lupe tried to console the boys.

For all their teenage bravado and prowess, they suddenly became so small to Natasha, and, as if they were young children, she kept them to a routine of supper, bath and bedtime, sitting with them until they had both fallen asleep. She sat watching them breathe for a good while before re-joining Mrs Puchetti in the living room.

Later that evening there was a commotion at the gate. The doorbell rang out like a fire alarm in the kitchen.

"Let me in! Let me in! It's Ed!"

He kicked at the iron grille on the gate and rang the bell again. Pedro opened the small door inset into the gate and Ed practically fell into his arms. He was crying, beside himself. Pedro half carried him into the living room.

"Sandy's dead, she's dead! A plane crash, what was she doing in a plane? What's going on?"

He sat heavily in an armchair, head in his hands, oblivious to the scene in the room. A sharp intake of breath drew Mrs Puchetti's attention to her daughter-in-law. Natasha sat with her mouth agape, her face contorted, she suddenly sat bolt upright.

"Of course! It was Sandy!" she said and turned to Ed. "Don't you see? Sam and Sandy were having an affair. They were together on that flight. They were going to Acapulco. It's all beginning to fall into place now. They must have been having an affair for months!"

Ed sat slack jawed, stunned as if each word she uttered was a blow to his stomach. He sounded winded as he let out a long, low moan, and then another and another as he began to rock back and forth, holding himself, containing himself as if he might shatter into a thousand pieces.

Mrs Puchetti, with Lupe's support, retired to her own room. She needed to be alone to address her grief head on. Lupe helped her brush her hair and get into her nightgown. She brought her a glass of warm milk with a shot of brandy in it to help her sleep. Meanwhile Ed and Natasha talked into the small hours. Somehow their mutual betrayal was a comfort. They compared notes, times, dates, lies. The grief was compounded by the deception.

"What do I say to the kids? How do they deal with this? How will they survive without their Mom?"

The enormity of the impact of this event was just dawning on Ed. It wasn't all about him. There were the kids, Sandy's parents, her sisters and brother, her nephews and nieces, her aunts and uncles, her cousins, her friends, her business partners. And this was just the human fallout. What about the housekeeping, shopping, meal planning, dealing with the maid, organising extra-curricular activities, chauffeuring the kids from dentist to doctor to art class to ballet to baseball practice, birthdays, Christmas, Easter and on and on and on. Right now, he could barely put one foot in front of another to make his way back next door to his sleeping children who were facing a dawn that would change their whole lives forever. Natasha offered to help him break the news to Heather and Jamie, even though she felt totally drained from having been through it with her own boys. And of course, the tricky question, the elephant in the room, the affair Sam and Sandy were having, how much of that should they divulge to the kids?

Mrs Puchetti was caught in a tsunami of grief and anger. She was at once devastated at her loss and so angry with Sam. What was he thinking? How could he do this to her and his children and poor Natasha?

Avenida de los Picos was shrouded in sadness. The parakeets, love birds and canaries at the Gantrys' house tweeted and cooed and fluttered about in their cages, unsettled by the fug of despair and cries of the neighbours on either side of their house. Mrs Puchetti changed her opinion of Mrs Gantry who was kindness itself. She made casseroles and pies and cookies for both grieving households, she offered to take Cha Cha and Harley for walks and teetered up the road in her leopard skin stilettos to the little park at the end of it, a leash in each hand, spectacles and necklaces bouncing off her chest as she panted to keep up with their pace. But most of all Mrs Gantry had the right words at the right time, especially for Mrs Puchetti. It turned out that the Gantrys had lost their only child to polio. It was before there was a vaccination, and the Gantrys always blamed themselves for taking their little girl to a public swimming pool in the swelter of the summer of 1952. They never got over the loss of their child and would not contemplate bringing another child into the world.

"It doesn't matter what age your child is when you lose them, the devastation is the same."

Mrs Gantry had invited Mrs Puchetti over to have tea in her garden to give her a break from the intensity generated by Natasha as she threw herself into funeral arrangements for Sam and spent as much time as she could cushioning the boys from the rawness of their loss.

"It makes no sense and doesn't follow the natural order of things. Mr Gantry and I couldn't bear to remain in the city which we felt was responsible for the death of our child. That's why we ended up living in Texas and then here, putting as much mileage as we could between ourselves and the place where we lost our child. But of course, she follows us wherever we are. The novelty of a new life soon wears off and you are left with the same sadness, the same longing and of course the memories of your cherished child."

Mrs Puchetti was not a stranger to loss. But this was like no other. Without Sam, her life had little meaning. Apart from her natural distress she was overcome with a cold fear for her future. Natasha wasn't likely to put up with caring for her into her dotage and any plans for her grandsons, the only link with her Sam, were entirely in her daughter-in-law's hands.

"Don't look at the big picture," soothed Mrs Gantry, "do what you need to do now, this hour, this afternoon. Everything else will gradually fall into place and you and Natasha will work out between you how your lives should proceed and most importantly what is best for your grandsons."

At this point, one of the canaries flew out from the living room into the garden and perched on Mrs Puchetti's walking stick.

"Oh my goodness! Hello little fellow! Aren't you a pretty boy!" she chuckled as Mrs Gantry tutted and cupped the bird in her hands.

"What are you doing out of your cage?" she cooed. "We must have left him hiding in the curtains at feeding time," she explained.

"He is so sweet. When he cheeps at me like that it is almost like he is a messenger from Sam coming to tell me everything will be all right!"

"Yes. Birds are remarkably sensitive to moods so I'm sure there's some truth in what you say."

It was the first time Mrs Puchetti had smiled in days and she left her neighbour's garden feeling a bit lighter and tapping out the mantra "take-it-one-step-at-a-time" with her walking stick as she did just that to her house next door.

Over the weeks that followed Ed and Natasha met up frequently to share what they knew about their spouses' infidelity and their feelings of abandonment and fury. Ed had had Sandy's body re-patriated to Texas and left her parents and siblings to make all the funeral arrangements. He drove himself and the children over the border and back again staying just one night with his in-laws. The funeral was an ordeal he had to endure for their sake, but he just felt numb. He was so wrapped up in his own distress he barely noticed how Heather and Jamie were handling their own loss. He stopped off at a shopping mall on the way home and filled the trunk of the car with toys and books and comics and new clothes for them. He turned up the radio when he heard one or other of them snivelling in the back seat and was relieved to hand them over to the attentions of the maid or the parents of their friends, so he didn't have to talk to them about their mother. Over the weeks they learned not to mention her too much in his presence. It was as if he was slowly erasing her from their lives, as if she never existed. They kept family photo albums in their bedrooms and shared their memories with each other, but there was no close adult around to help them process their grief. Heather's grades slipped and Jamie's behaviour in school became an issue, but this just compounded their father's fury and his determination to get away and start again.

"One thing's for sure Nat," Ed confided as they shared a beer on the Puchetti patio. "There's no way I'm staying here, in the house, in our life without her. I feel as if I'm suffocating. Everything that surrounds me and the sheer exhaustion of dealing with everyday stuff just reminds me of her absence. I need to re-set my life with Heather and Jamie and take us the hell outta here."

"I feel just the same, but I think it's too soon for my boys to pull them out of their routine with school and all their extra-curricular stuff in the middle of the year. Sam and I were always planning to send them back stateside to complete high school. We had already decided which boarding school would be best and we'd picked one near my family so at least they could go stay with my sister for the odd weekend. I need to talk to Eva. There's so much to decide. She's lost so much already, but I can't see myself staying here and I have to put myself and the boys ahead of her needs I'm afraid. Have you decided where you will go?"

"Well, my work has offices in Miami and there's an opening for me there. I've got a realtor on the lookout for a house, but we'll just rent in the meantime. At least the compensation and insurance will ease the burden of re-locating and kids are kids. They'll make new friends in no time."

Natasha understood where Ed was coming from. It was hard to talk to her boys about their "wonderful" father, but she tried to rise above her own feelings and join them in remembering what a good dad he was and the great memories they had made as a family. Photos of better times were framed and hung on the walls of their bedrooms and she was lucky to have Mrs Puchetti to help comfort them in their sorrow.

As the eulogy was read at Sam's funeral by his best friend, Natasha sat in the pew flanked by her mother-in-law and Gregorio, barely able to contain her rage.

"He was a generous, kind man, a family man, a rock to his wife, his mother and his two fine sons," droned on Octavio, looking towards their pew.

"He was a liar, a cheat, a fake!" screamed Natasha in her head. "He made my whole life a lie. Everything I thought was solid and secure is dust!"

As if she could hear the wailing inside her head, Mrs Puchetti grasped Natasha's hand and held it tight, to anchor her through the remainder of the service. Lupe sat in the pew behind the family with Pedro, Arturo, Cousin Gustavo and Aurora. Lupe had made sure everything was ready back at the house for the wake. She and Pedro had spent the morning preparing food and setting out cutlery, crockery and glasses. Cakes and sweetmeats had been delivered by the local bakery and cold drinks and wine were stored in the fridge. Lupe changed into her more formal uniform when they returned home, and she and Pedro circulated amongst the guests with trays of drinks and canapés. Sam had lots of friends, some of whom Natasha had never met before today, highlighting the chasm between their two lives, and of course he had never met some of the friends she had made on her courses and from her women's group. By late afternoon most of the mourners had returned home to their normal lives leaving the Puchetti household to get on with the slow business of coming to terms with their loss.

Confession

Esther switched off the radio and plonked herself next to her mother on her bed.

"I have to tell you something. It's very hard because I know you will be upset, but you need to know that something terrible has happened to Sandy and Sam."

Esther gazed uncomprehending at her mother.

"What? Sandy? Sam? Why? What's happened?"

She started to cry, and Rose held her in her arms for a few minutes.

"Here," said Rose, unfolding the letter, "you better read this."

Esther read and re-read the letter. It was from Mrs Puchetti describing the circumstances around her son's death, the funeral and how Natasha and the boys were coping with it all. A newspaper clipping was included with the letter reporting on the fate of the flight to Acapulco. Esther shook her head in disbelief as she read it:

... Only two survivors walked away from the carnage without so much as a scratch. Interviewed by Radio Ciudad they recounted the horror of the last few minutes of the flight. Everything was as normal, maybe a bit of turbulence after take-off. Suddenly the plane began to shudder and pitch and then slowly, slowly, it began to lose altitude. There was a flurry of activity as the air hostess bowled into the cockpit. She emerged shouting "put you heads down like this!" demonstrating the emergency position. The plane plunged out of the sky and skidded for several hundred yards. A crack formed along the length of the aircraft as it ploughed through a farmer's field. The plane filled with foul, oozing mud. Anyone who survived the impact was suffocated by the mud which filled their ears, their mouths and their nostrils ...

She saw their names there in print on the passenger list. Sandra Roberts and Samuel Puchetti, both of Lomas, Mexico City.

"Oh Mom! How awful! I knew! I knew!" she blubbered as her mother held her in her arms.

"You knew what?" Rose asked, surprised at her daughter's words.

"I knew and I didn't tell anyone. If I'd only said something this would never have happened!!"

Rose hesitated.

"You knew about Sam and Sandy? But how?"

Esther confessed to her mother about her illicit afternoon with Zac in Chapultepec Park, about what she had seen, about how she had felt for Heather, about how she had felt she had to keep it secret.

Rose hugged her tight.

"I am so, so sorry my poor darling. I'm sorry you had to go through that on your own. I knew too you know."

Esther looked at her mother.

"You did?"

"Yes, Sandy told me, she had no one else she could confide in. You have absolutely nothing to blame yourself for, Esther, nothing whatsoever. Sam and Sandy were adults who knew exactly what they were doing and what the risks were. It was their choice. Nothing you or I could have said or done would have changed anything. It is very, very sad, it's tragic and I know how upset you are for Heather."

"What will I say to her?"

"I'm sure anything you say will be the right thing. You're a good friend, you'll find the right words."

Esther forgot about her French homework. She sat down to write the most difficult letter of her life. Three months later she received a reply.

689 Glebe Street

Myrtle Beach

Florida

Valentine's Day!!

Hiya Est!

A lot has happened since my last letter. As you can see, we've moved to Florida! It is sooooooo groovy here and I'm having a blast. I'm seeing this boy call Tony and ... wait for it ... he drives a red T bird!!! He is so boss, the ultimate! We've been going steady practically since we moved here. Dad doesn't approve (of course, what's new?), but where there's love there's a way! I don't miss Mexico one little bit. Since you left everyone was so boring, same old people, same old lessons, same old parties. I'm so glad to be back in the groove again in the good old US of A! I've bought LOADS of new clothes and isn't it cool we can listen to all the number ones whilst they are actually still in the charts. Mexico seems so old fashioned to me now. I have made some really groovy friends and get on really well with this chick called Lesley Ann. She has peroxided her hair AND IS ON THE PILL! The other day we made brownies with you-know-what!! We got so high I couldn't stop laughing! Wish you were with me.

Love,

Your pal 4 ever,

Heather

Esther read her friend's letter trying to find something of Heather in it, something recognisable that she could hold on to, but she could not sense her friend between the lines this stranger had written.

"She doesn't even mention her mother!" Esther said, sitting on the couch next to Rose. She blew her nose and plucked several tissues from the box on the coffee table.

"She's still reeling from the shock of her mother's death," soothed Rose. "She is blocking it totally from her mind because it is far too painful for her to deal with right now."

"But she has a new best friend and she's turning into one of those fast girls."

"I know how painful it is for you, my love, but you have to accept that Heather is getting on with her life as best she can, and you have to do the same. You do know that when we go back for our visit it won't be the same as it was before. People will have moved away or changed schools or found new friends. I believe Gregorio and Giovanni are still living with their grandmother, but chances are they will soon be sent away to school here in the US."

Esther pondered this.

"I guess so. I'm already not the same as I was before, am I?"

"It's called growing up, and you are doing it beautifully."

"At least Mrs Puchetti and Cha Cha will still be there!"

By June the Puchettis had settled into a kind of routine that didn't include Sam. Natasha was surprised at how smooth this transition was and realised that not much had changed. Sam had been absent both physically and emotionally, detached from the family, from her, for a very long time and in reality, it had been down to her to run the household and see to the arrangements for the boys.

"The nights are the worst. When everything is quiet and I'm left to my own thoughts in that big bed, that's when my mind starts to race. I've never realised so many conflicting emotions could be felt at the same time. Rage, sadness and just blind fear keep me awake for hours," Natasha says, sitting in the living room of one of her friends from the women's group.

Its Moira's turn to host it. Unlike most of the group, Moira lives in a large apartment on Mariano Escobedo. It is in a modern block and has floor-to-ceiling windows along the back living room wall and there is a door which opens on to a patio decked in gay ceramic pots of flowers and larger clay urns housing ferns and a banana tree. The living room is bathed in light and the women sit on comfortable sofas and armchairs each embellished with scatter cushions, most of which are Moira's own needlepoint creations.

The group has become an anchor of sanity for Natasha, and she looks forward to their weekly meetings. Since Sam's death each of the women have comforted and inspired her in different ways. Madi encourages her with her writing whilst Geraldine is able to share the experience of loss. Moira offers practical advice, having been through a divorce herself, and can recommend financial advisors and lawyers to handle Sam's estate. Natasha feels like she has a team on her side rooting for her from the side-lines.

Dorothy stirs her tea, taking in what Natasha is saying.

"When you say fear, can you put your finger on what you are afraid of?"

"Nothing and everything. My mind just jumps from one thing to another. The boys, Eva, the house, the car, the dog, the bills, school, appointments. You name it, the thoughts come unbidden and before I know it its 4 am and then I worry about not getting enough sleep to cope with all these things the next day."

Dorothy nods.

"You see when you have a trauma, a shock like you have had, everything is magnified. Feelings are numbed for a period and then, wham! Suddenly you're drowning in a tidal wave of mixed emotions. Problems which you would normally deal with and tick off your to-do list suddenly seem insurmountable. A dirty sock found under a bed, separated from its pair which has already been laundered and folded and put into the drawer can be the trigger of huge rage, seeming like the last straw in a sequence of last straws that you are having to deal with."

"True," pipes up Laura. "You need to be kind to yourself. You don't need to be superwoman. Forget all the minutiae. They will all come good and if they don't it's not the end of the world. So long as your boys are as settled as they can be and you can gradually sort out the immediate practicalities, the house, your mother-in-law, the dog and so on will just have to take a back seat for now."

Natasha feels like a kid who has been told they don't have to do their homework. Laura is right. Not everything has to be made perfect right now. She can give herself permission to take her time. She resolves to follow other advice her friends give her. Prioritise the important stuff that can't wait and forget the dirty odd sock. It will soon find its way into the laundry and be reunited with its pair in the drawer.

Mrs Puchetti and Natasha are in the offices of Sam's lawyer Señor Gomez Diezcanedo. The office is in the same building as Sam's architectural firm, and it seems strange entering this building in order to have his last will and testament read to them rather than meeting him to go for lunch or pre-theatre drinks. *Diezcanedo Abogado* is etched into the window of the office door, and they are shown into a cool room, tastefully decorated, with bookshelves lined with lawbooks and three desks piled high with files and folders.

Diezcanedo smokes a pipe and shuffles through the paperwork before withdrawing the document he needs.

"Ah yes," he looks over his half-moon spectacles at the two ladies sitting before him.

"First, may I offer my sincere condolences for the loss of your dear son and husband," he says, nodding at Mrs Puchetti and Natasha in turn. "You know I held Sam in high regard, and I hope I will continue to be at your service with any matters that may concern you."

He cleared his throat and tapped out the tobacco from his pipe into an ashtray. The whole office was in a fug of *Balkan Sobranie*. Natasha wished she could open a window, but Mrs Puchetti quite liked the smell. It reminded her of her Rafael.

"Now then, the will is very straightforward, and you probably know most of it anyway. As you know Sam's assets, besides the amounts he held in his bank accounts, consist of a third share in Puchetti's Ice Cream, and a third share in the architectural company Montes, Ortiz y Puchetti. On top of this there is the very considerable compensation payment from the Airline company and of course the pay-out from the life insurance plan he had. Mr Puchetti has left the shares in both companies to you Natasha and you should benefit also from the monies left in his bank accounts and the pay-outs. Eva, you have your third share in Puchetti's Ice Cream which brings you a reasonable income and your husband provided for you with your entitlement to half his pension and the monthly life insurance payment which I believe you receive?"

Mrs Puchetti nods in agreement.

"You also are the sole owner of the property in which the family resides, yes?"

Mrs Puchetti again nods assent, the colour rising in her cheeks and tears welling up in her eyes. She takes a hankie from the cuff of her blouse and dabs her eyes. Natasha reaches over to put a reassuring hand on her arm.

Mr Diezcanedo smiles at them kindly.

"I know how difficult this is ... so much administration at a time when people are most vulnerable after losing a loved one. But Sam has provided very well for all of you. There are also the children's bonds he purchased when the boys were born and coincidentally these will mature in October. There is sufficient there to cover school and college fees so you will not need to worry on that score Natasha."

Natasha had forgotten about the bonds. Sam saw to all the financial side of things – bills, savings and so on. It was beginning to dawn on her that she would have to get pretty savvy pretty quickly when it came to all things financial. The rest of the meeting was taken up with discussing her options with regards to her share of the ice cream business and arranging a future meeting once Montes, Ortiz y Puchetti sent him the documents he needed regarding Sam's pension and the share certificate.

The Lunch

Mrs Puchetti and Natasha go to Sanborns for lunch after the meeting with Diezcanedo. They feel they should mark Sam's final wishes through the reading of the will with a nice lunch. The architecture of Sanborns and the beautiful columns and ceramic wall and floor tiles which surround the tables make this a fitting place to celebrate him. He had been a talented architect and his clients appreciated how he incorporated the colonial with the modern in houses that had special features harking back to colonial times. The women ordered lunch and sipped their iced water, taking in the majesty of the building before Mrs Puchetti broke the silence.

"This might be a good time for us to have a talk about things, while we have a quiet moment together and without the boys around."

Natasha sipped from her glass and nodded.

"I have spent a great deal of time over the last few weeks admiring how wonderfully you are coping with everything that has happened, Natasha. You have remained calm and level-headed and been such a comfort to the boys and me even though I am sure inside you are full of so many conflicting feelings."

Tears came immediately to Natasha and she hurriedly opened her pocketbook and withdrew some tissues with which she dabbed the corners of her eyes. Mrs Puchetti waited for Natasha to ride this surge of emotion and poured her daughter-in-law some more water from the pitcher.

"I'm so sorry! Natasha finally gasped. Gosh! That came out of left field."

She took another sip of water and composed her features.

"It's just that I'm just about functioning, but a kind word here or there can just set me off! Do not be deceived by this calm exterior," she continued, circling her face with her finger.

"Underneath I'm a Popocatépetl of every emotion under the sun and could erupt at any time!"

Mrs Puchetti smiled and reached over the table to press her hand into Natasha's cheek.

"You do not need to apologise to me! What can I say? I miss my boy, but I cannot judge him. In spite of his ridiculous behaviour with that woman, above all I know he loved you and nothing was more important to him than his family. Marriages are all unique, yours was unique, and why Sam felt he had to risk losing it all is inexplicable! So she flattered him, so he felt desired. After the first flush they would have seen sense. Flattering stops and desire fades and in the end it's what you have in common and the history you share that counts. You think, other than the excitement of having a bit on the side that those two had anything in common? NO! His head was turned, and he had lost his way with you. You both led such busy lives there was not room to re-connect with what drew you together in the first place. I hope one day you can forgive my Sammy, who, granted, was an absolute fool, and think back with gladness for the good life and wonderful sons you two made together."

Natasha hung on every word her mother-in-law uttered. Could it be that this had been no more than a fling? Was Sam in love with Sandy, or more with the idea of being "in love"? She would never really know. After his death she had been obsessed with finding evidence of his infidelity. She tore through his bookcases, leafing through every book looking for a note or letter. His desk drawers were emptied, his wardrobe raided with every pocket in every suit and jacket searched. His diary was dissected with hidden meanings suspected behind every abbreviation which wasn't obvious. SXOCH had her guessing until she realised it meant Sandy Xochimilco written in the date of that particular tryst. She remembers tearing the page into tiny pieces and throwing it down the toilet whilst screaming "YOU FUCKING BASTARD!!!".

For all its size and grandeur, the walls of the house were sucking the air out of her. She couldn't sit in one room for any length of time without settling her gaze on an ornament, a photo, a piece of artwork that she and Sam had collected around them to make this their home. It was the Puchetti residence when he brought her to Mexico after their wedding. Even though her mother-in-law had insisted she and Sam decorate and reconfigure the layout to their own specifications to suit their family needs, in reality, this had never really been her home. And now?

Almost as if she could read Natasha's thoughts Mrs Puchetti continued.

"I suppose you too must be wondering what next? I know I have been thinking about little else. To be blunt, apart from you and the boys I have no-one. I haven't seen my sister since we left Italy and rarely hear from her, other than the odd letter bemoaning her fate and complaining about the taxes she has to pay on my father's little piece of land. She wants me to feel guilty, but she has benefitted from the bounty of the nut and olive trees and built up a good little business with her husband. I have no intention of ever returning to Italy. This is my home and here I will see out my days. But this is your home too, Natasha, and nothing would make me happier than for you and the boys to remain."

"That's kind of you Eva," Natasha clenched her serviette in her fists and swallowed hard, trying to keep the tears at bay. She had made enough of a spectacle of herself already.

"But I want to make one thing perfectly clear," continued Mrs Puchetti. "I am not your responsibility Natasha. You are still young enough to start a new life, maybe one day find a new love, have a career, become a great writer! Whatever you decide you know you will have my love and support."

Natasha smiled at her mother-in-law and leaned in towards her. Now was the time to divulge what she had in reality more or less already decided about her future.

"Well, you know that Sam and I had planned to send the boys to the States next year to finish school. In fact, we had even chosen a school which has a good academic record and plenty of sport and extra-curricular activities quite near to where my family live. We figured they could spend the odd weekend or holiday with my parents or sister and Christmas and the Summer back here with us."

"Yes," Eva said, "Sam did tell me of your plans. It would be a huge wrench for them, and me! But I suppose given the new circumstances, without their father to keep them in check, the school would keep them occupied and on an even keel."

Natasha tried not to feel miffed at the assumption she couldn't cope on her own with the raising of her fatherless sons. But she did actually realise that she seemed to be having less influence on them and had lately been relying more and more on Sam to lay down the law and deal with raucous, selfish, and at times insolent adolescent behaviour. "Wait till you father gets home!" was a cliché she had never had to have recourse to, until the last year or so.

Mrs Puchetti finished her prawn and avocado cocktail and carefully placed the little silver fish fork on her plate, daintily wiping the corners of her mouth with the linen serviette.

"And what about you? Have you had any thoughts about what you will do when they go away?"

Natasha had given a great deal of thought about her future without Sam, without the boys, on her own in the house which was never her home. And she recognised that no matter how much her mother-in-law and she cared for one another, they were from different worlds and often rubbed each other up the wrong way. She had spent the last session at her women's group talking about her options. Her friends had helped her clarify what she wanted from this new widowed version of herself. They had pooled their collective thoughts and knowledge and it emerged that Natasha wanted to return to the States when the boys started school there. She wanted to find a house near her family and the boys' boarding school so she could have regular contact and she would try to find some freelance writing for local newspapers and magazines. She also decided to enrol on an extra-mural creative writing course at the local college.

Madi had also added helpfully: "I know it's too soon but finding someone new will be easier there. This place is too much like a goldfish bowl. Everyone knows your business. You aren't ready now, but one day you may well want to meet someone new."

Now was the time to tell Mrs Puchetti her plans. The waiter brought them plates and placed a platter of chicken mole, a basket of warm tortillas and a bowl each of guacamole and sour cream on their table. They tucked into their meal and ate in companionable silence for a few minutes.

"This is nice. But Lupe makes better mole than this, don't you think?"

Mrs Puchetti nodded.

"We are so lucky to have her and Pedro, aren't we?"

Natasha nodded as she refilled their water glasses.

"What would you do though Eva, if I were also to move back home to the States. How would you manage?"

Mrs Puchetti had a ready answer.

"Don't you fret about me! I may be old, but I have all my marbles and can make my own decisions about my future. I do have an idea which I have shared with Sam's friend Gustavo. He seemed the right person to approach about this before I consult with Lupe and Pedro, just to sound him out seeing as he knows Lupe's family and their circumstances. I am very fond of Lupe and Pedro, and of course I have adored Arturo since the day he was born. But before I make any decisions about my future, I need to have your blessing, Natasha. I would like them to continue living here with me."

"That makes sense. No one knows better how to run the household and of course Lupe is very devoted to you."

"I am going to propose that they take over the upper floor of the house. I am getting too stiff to manage the stairs. The new extension will suit my purposes. There is plenty of room upstairs for them to make a nice home for themselves especially if they decide to have another child, and there will still be room for you and the boys when you come for a visit. I realise that there won't be as much to do with just me here, but I'm happy for Lupe and Pedro to find other part-time work that fits in with their routine here. Meanwhile I will have the security of knowing they are here and looking after me."

"It would certainly make me feel easier leaving you if I knew they were here watching over you," Natasha said, in fact, she felt that a great weight had been lifted from her. She wouldn't be able to contemplate her and the boys' future move to the States unless she knew someone was looking after her mother-in-law. And now here she was offering her a "get out of jail free" card.

"Well, that's settled then. Now I just need to discuss this fully with Lupe and Pedro. There is a lot for them to take into consideration, not least her concerns about her mother. But you should know that in return for their loyalty I shall be adjusting my will. I hope this is okay with you, Natasha. When I die, I shall be leaving them one third of the proceeds of the sale of the residence and the car. The other two thirds and the rest of my estate will of course go to Gregorio and Giovanni. I would like you to have my jewellery and any of the paintings and antiques you want. Perhaps we should do some kind of inventory over the next few weeks just to see what's what. And we can also have a big clear-out!"

At Margarita's

Margarita is watering the tomatoes on her patio when Gustavo's car pulls up on the road outside. He is accompanied by Lupe, Pedro and Arturo and they call out their greetings as they enter the little kitchen and emerge onto the patio. Gustavo had planned this Sunday excursion with Lupe and Pedro, and they were more than happy to take full advantage of a ride in his nice car, forsaking the long and bumpy bus ride out of the city and into the countryside. Margarita has been expecting them and has prepared a light lunch and fresh lemonade which is laid out on the kitchen table. Miguel Ángel arrives home at the same time and they all take up their places around the kitchen table with Gustavo at the head in the captain's chair. The previously gloomy kitchen is now well lit with a neon strip ceiling light and the plastic sunflower tablecloth has been replaced with one gaily covered in red and green poinsettias.

Lupe is pleased to see her mother looking more robust as she bustles around her kitchen before settling with a satisfied smile at the table with her family. The family bring each other up to date on all their news.

"It's so good of you, Gustavo, to come to see me. I know how busy you are at work. Aurora is well?"

"Yes. She is fine. I left her to send out some invoices which are long overdue. She sends her love and promises to come next time."

"Well, it is lovely to see you, all of you!" she laughs, bursting with happiness at this unexpected reunion. After all she had only seen Lupe a few weeks ago and wasn't really due another visit from her for a month or so.

Once the meal has been consumed, Arturo wanders off to feed the chickens and pick some strawberries from the pots on his grandmother's patio. Gustavo adjusts his spectacles on his nose and clears his throat, commanding everyone's attention.

"I have to confess to an ulterior motive for arranging this visit Margarita, lovely though it is to catch up on all the latest news with all of you."

"This sounds rather formal, Gustavo," Margarita's consternation is etched in the furrows of her forehead. "Is something wrong?"

"Not at all!" Gustavo pats his cousin's arm reassuringly. "I have what I hope is good news for all of us. Mrs Puchetti has sent me here on a mission."

"Mrs Puchetti? Are we losing our jobs?" Lupe looks alarmed.

"*Cálmate*! It's nothing like that!" Gustavo chuckles. "On the contrary. Mrs Puchetti has a proposal to put to you, but she didn't want to put you under any pressure to accept by meeting with you face to face."

"Well, what is it?" Pedro draws his chair in and clasps his hands on top of the tablecloth.

"As you both know there are soon to be big changes with the Puchetti family,"

Lupe and Pedro nod sadly.

"The Señora and the boys will be moving to the United States in September leaving the old lady on her own. She would very much like it if you, Lupe and Pedro would stay on to look after her and the house."

Lupe and Pedro exchange glances in disbelief. Have they heard correctly?

"What she proposes is a very generous package which will give you security in your jobs and set you up for the future. You and Arturo will occupy the upper storey of the house and make it your home. She recognises that there will not be as much for you both to do with just her living there, but is happy for you to take on other part-time work as you wish. In exchange you will take care of the affairs of the house and look after her if and when she is less capable of looking after herself."

Lupe and Pedro's faces mirror each other, their mouths agape, eyes wide open as they take in Gustavo's words.

"Furthermore, she proposes leaving you both one third of the proceeds from the sale of the property upon her death in recognition of your hard work and loyalty."

Lupe gasps and puts a hand over her mouth to stifle a cry. She looks to her mother who is beaming and squeezing Gustavo's arm.

"*Dios mío*! I wasn't expecting anything like this! Pedro and I knew that change was coming but we were preparing for the worst-case scenario!"

Pedro put an arm around Lupe's shoulder and drew her towards him, planting a kiss on her cheek. "I don't know what to say!"

Margarita claps her hands with glee.

"Say how wonderful *mi vida*! It is no more than you both deserve! You have served that family well and this is your reward!"

Margarita makes everyone laugh as she stands and does a little dance right there on the kitchen tiles, clapping her hands over her head. Gustavo stands and grabbing her 'round the waist, waltzes her out to the patio, turns, and tangoes her back into the kitchen, taking up his position in the captain's chair chortling to himself and wiping his brow with his handkerchief.

"Ehem!" order is restored. "However, there is something else I need to discuss with you my dear cousin. You do not have to give me an answer right away but please do consider this seriously. Given that Lupe will now be permanently based in the city, Aurora and I would like you and Miguel Ángel to come and live with us. We have more than enough room, Aurora will appreciate the company and I would like to take Miguel Ángel on as an apprentice."

It's as if an electric current has run through Miguel Ángel's body. He sits bolt upright in his chair.

"You mean work for you? In the photography studio?"

"You will finish school this summer and will be looking for a job, no? My business means everything to me, and I would like to think that I can pass it on to my family when I am too decrepit to hang around Chapultepec and stand for long hours in the dark room. I will teach you everything I know and pay you a wage. What do you say?"

Margarita could no longer stem the flood of tears. It was all too much! All this good news was almost beyond belief. Miguel Ángel rose from his chair and went round the table to where his uncle was sitting. He held out his hand in a manly handshake.

"Thank you, Gustavo, for doing me this honour!"

Miguel Ángel looked so serious and sounded so earnest that everyone laughed. Margarita looked at her family gathered in one place and felt a deep sense of peace that they would no longer be separated. The sunset that evening was glorious, and the family sang and danced into the night, bathed in the light from a full moon which cast its silvery glow onto Margarita's patio.

Changes

In the months that followed Sam's death Mrs Puchetti prepared herself for great changes in her life. Conversations around boarding school and removal arrangements for Natasha and her grandsons were a welcome distraction from those about Sam and Sandy. What to take and what to leave behind for vacation stays were discussed at length over the dinner table leaving Mrs Puchetti exhausted and in need of a siesta. The constants in her life were Lupe, Pedro and Arturo, a few friends (the ones that were still alive!) and strangely Mrs Gantry.

Over this painful time Mrs Gantry had time and again been a comfort to Mrs Puchetti. Beneath the animal print tops, stiletto sandals and her sparkly jewels, bangles and hair combs, Mrs Gantry was kindness itself and she spent many an hour with her neighbour listening to her as she poured out her grief and shared memories of her son. She had helped her sort out her box of photographs into albums, painstakingly sticking down little white corners and sliding the photos in. Whilst doing this they chatted about their lives and Mrs Puchetti was struck by how much they had in common through the struggles they had endured and the times through which they had lived, but also through their shared sense of humour. Mrs Gantry could at times be rather risqué and Mrs Puchetti hid her face but rocked with laughter with some of the things she came out with, especially about men.

In late June a removal truck pulled up outside the gates and three burly men spent the day going back and forth to the house carrying boxes and furniture. Natasha sat exhausted on the porch watching her life go out of the gate. The packers had been there for three days and she had carefully labelled every box and used a different colour marker for each room they were to go into at the end of their journey into the house she had rented in Boston. The boys had already been dispatched to her sister's so that they weren't in the way as Natasha helped her mother-in-law sort the house out.

The new extension was ideal for Mrs Puchetti with a large bedroom, dressing room and bathroom, another spacious room which could be for the boys when they visited and a smaller room which could be a study and double up as a room for Natasha on her visits. Finally, it was time for Natasha to leave. Her women's group held a *despedida* for her, inviting people she had befriended on her many courses as well as those longer-term friends from when the boys were small. Madi made a lovely speech and Mrs Puchetti cried. On the day of her departure, at Natasha's request, Mrs Gantry came over so that her mother-in-law wouldn't be alone when she left. Together with Lupe, Pedro and Arturo they stood at the roadside as Natasha loaded her suitcase into the waiting taxi and then, choking back tears, embraced each one in turn with a special abrazo and kisses for her mother-in-law. Mrs Gantry put her arm around her friend's shoulder. They all waved until the taxi disappeared around the corner.

"That's that! Mrs Puchetti's small frame was wracked by sobs. Mrs Gantry coaxed her back into the garden to sit on the patio. Lupe went to make them some tea. Cha Cha barked excitedly knowing something was up.

"*Ya basta* Cha Cha! Come here!"

The dog padded over to Mrs Puchetti and lay companionably at her feet.

Mrs Puchetti distracted herself by turning all her attention and energies into helping Lupe and Pedro plan and transform their new quarters into a home. The smell of fresh paint and polished floors filled the house as they took up residence in the upper storey. The large master bedroom with its balcony which overlooked the garden became their living room and they luxuriated in the additional three bedrooms and bathroom which would take them several months to furnish. Pedro spent all his free time fixing shelves and building cupboards. Arturo's room had plenty of space for all the toys he had inherited from Gregorio and Giovanni. He especially felt the absence of the boys and his friends, but Pedro kept him busy with chores and helping in the garden when he was not otherwise occupied with school and homework. One of the smaller bedrooms was being transformed into a nursery and much time off was spent at Sears Robuck choosing items of nursery furniture for it. Before going to bed at night Lupe took great pleasure in peering into the room, inhaling the smell of fresh paint and gently caressing the new baby clothes and the baby blanket that Margarita had crocheted. Mrs Puchetti insisted on buying the crib and bedding and Gustavo and Aurora contributed a lovely rocking chair and a big teddy bear. Mrs Puchetti had been delighted with the news of this little addition to the household. It was a great distraction having something to look forward to and she absorbed herself in knitting little booties and bonnets in preparation for the birth. She confined her grieving to the evenings when the house was quiet and there were no interruptions. Then she would think of her son and her husband, rocking back and forth in her chair, hugging herself and crying silently so as not to disturb the sleeping household.

The following May, Lupe delivered a beautiful baby girl and, much to Mrs Puchetti's delight, they named her Emilia Samanta Luz. Lupe and Pedro took it in turns to care for her as they had with Arturo but Mrs Puchetti too had her time with the new baby, singing old Italian lullabies and rocking her in her cradle on the patio next to her. She never tired of looking at her tiny face and all the funny little contortions of her eyes and nose and mouth as she slept. The party after the baptism was held in the garden. Margarita came over early to help with the food and Jesús travelled down from their village to be with all the family. Miguel Ángel showed Arturo how to use his camera and helped him take photographs as all the adults caught up with family news and took it in turns to admire the baby.

Esther sits at her desk by a large sash window. Being on the third floor of her apartment block she looks down on a walled communal garden . It stretches behind the six mansion blocks which line this side of the road, a little haven in the middle of the metropolis. She is like one of the birds in the beautiful oak and ash trees that frame her view , looking down on the lawn and shrubs and watching the squirrels leap from branch to branch and along the garden wall. Esther's life has been squeezed into the confines of her apartment during this year of global pandemic. The seasonal changes in the garden have been a constant source of pleasure and a reminder of the passage of time as she observes it from above. Today as the trees are on the cusp of bursting forth in blossom and the tulips in her flower bed once again open like a row of ballerinas in their crimson tutus, Esther remembers a garden from her youth . She fiddles with the silver bracelet which hangs heavy on her wrist. Over the years she has added to the charms she had received as a girl from Mrs Puchetti. Her wedding day is represented by a silver olive tree whilst her grandchildren's tiny hand or footprints have been etched into four small silver discs with each of their names on the back. Esther has spent this year of enforced separation counting her blessings whilst at the same time nursing an underlying melancholy and reminiscing about her life, about her parents , now long gone, and her childhood. The little dog on the bracelet reminds her of Cha Cha.

The last time Esther had seen Mrs Puchetti was on a family visit to Mexico in 1968. She had invited the family to tea and as they stepped into the garden, Esther's heart ached for the happy times she had spent there. Mrs Puchetti looked the same, but her hair was now completely white and she spoke slowly, weighing each word before releasing it into the still, warm air that separated her from her guests. Inevitably the conversation had turned to the family tragedy. Mrs Puchetti frequently wiped her eyes with an embroidered hankie which she slipped from the cuff of her sleeve. Esther remembers sitting with her sisters under the palm tree with Arturo and his little sister whilst the grown-ups caught up with their news. Esther looked up at the sun-drenched bougainvillea which trailed from the balcony and listened to the shriek of a peacock in a nearby garden. The lizards darted in and out of the shrubbery sunning themselves on the garden wall. She remembers thinking that everything was the same and yet nothing was the same. Life was fragile, unpredictable, and in a few weeks she herself would travel to London to study at university. Her life in New York would become as much of a dream as this now was, here in Mrs Puchetti's garden. She would follow in the wake of Lupe and Mrs Puchetti and her mother, Rose, charting her own waters into adulthood in a foreign place and on her own.

Esther sighs and unclasps the bracelet, laying it on her desk. She opens her laptop and types "Avenida de Los Picos" into the search engine. She is immediately transported to the street in Lomas. There is the blue of the Mexican sky and the deep purple of the bougainvillea shrubs which adorn some of the gateposts of the houses. There is her house, still recognisable, with its balcony and red tiled roof. She moves the cursor and travels down the street. The jacaranda trees have matured and obscure her view of some of the houses. She stops at the spot where Mrs Puchetti's house should be, but a modern white apartment block seems to have sprung up in its place. All that remains of Mrs. Puchetti's garden is the palm tree whose fronds now tower above the garden wall, seemingly bent by a soft breeze, as if waving a final farewell.